Junctions Of Life

Lessons you can benefit from . . .

Anthony S B Ng

PARTRIDGE
A Penguin Random House Company

To order additional copies of this book, contact
Toll Free 800 101 2657 (Singapore)
Toll Free 1 800 81 7340 (Malaysia)
orders.singapore@partridgepublishing.com

www.partridgepublishing.com/singapore

Contents

Acknowledgement

It would not have been possible for "Junctions Of Life" to see the light of day, had it not been for the urging, encouragement and support that my beloved family and my many friends had given me in my first attempt to author a book.

Most of all I owe it to Almighty Father for His divine intervention, in guiding me through this journey, which for a non cerebral individual like me, would have been a humongous if not impossible task struggling to compose an essay, much less write a book.

To my lovely wife, Betty for her selflessness in putting up with my idiosyncracies and yet full of motivation in helping me put pen to paper.

To my lovely children, Cheryl, Don and Earlene for their persistent urging and encouragement to journalise the events that shaped our lives for the benefit of others.

To the many friends who in one way or other contributed their takes on what could be lessons in life, especially Cheng Huang Leng who readily agreed, over dinner, to allow me to reproduce wholesale his personal experience on "How To Retire."

To the many mentors and *"mentors"* who shaped my experiences in my life.

This book was written not to disparage anyone but the encounters provided relevant learning curves for people in general, on how to manage oneself.

I hope you will enjoy my anecdotal interpretations.

I liken one's life to a journey, as we travel through time with many encounters at each stop on the way. This is where one discovers many things, meets people from all walks of life, visits many places of interest, and tastes the many foods such destinations have to offer. Our interactions with all these would in one way or another offer us important lessons that will set the stage for our outlook on life. One can harvest rich experiences from these encounters that would offer valuable lessons on good practices, habits, styles, and behaviour that we can choose to adopt and adapt, while others we can choose to ignore or avoid.

Without exception, everyone will have many junctions to cross throughout the course of one's lifetime. Some are Godsend; others are manmade. While the former are quite beyond our control, the latter require some decisions to be made, and hopefully this book will offer some tips to help readers make the correct decisions.

Every stop, junction, or crossroads will shape and change us. It is important to ponder at these junctions and never walk back. By all means look back for the lessons, but never walk back, as life is progressive, not regressive. Learn from the past, and move on. What the future holds for us is for us to make. Life is what you make of it.

What follows is a narration of the encounters many of my friends have contributed on their journeys. Hopefully these will, in one way or another, help us better manage our own. My role here is really to aggregate the sharing in writing for the benefit of all. For ease of reference, the common and central characters are Dean and his wife, Bridget, who will assume the many roles for the many junctions as they travelled through the journeys that all these friends have contributed.

The First Junction

It was a hot weekend afternoon. Dean's mother was busy baking cakes for the coming Chinese New Year. Dad was busy helping spring clean their humble compound atap hut (an olden-style house with a roof thatched with dried leaves from the atap trees, which are commonly found among mangrove trees along the coast of Singapore), which was located in Choa Chu Kang. Everyone was busy with one thing or another, as usual during that time of year, preparing to usher in the Chinese New Year.

Dean was seven years old and had a sticky tendency to ape his older siblings. Cousin Kenny, having been in the school's scout movement, was eager to show off his newly acquired skills in building a tree house. In the huge village compound was a star fruit tree. Kenny and Dean's older brother, Danny, built a tree house, made up of only several discarded planks of wood, affixed with ropes. They had with them small penknives, water and salt, and some receptacles for their use. The lower-hanging fruits were theirs for the picking. There they were, totally immersed in their activities and oblivious to the fact that poor Dean was just below them, straining his neck and pleading with them to allow him to climb up to the tree house to join them. They did not bother, let alone acknowledge his presence. After a few pleadings and what seemed like an eternity to Dean, he was very upset that his pleas fell on deaf ears. Compounding his anguish was the fact that he was dealing with none other than his own brother and first cousin. He began back-stepping, his eyes still affixed on the two, hoping for some eye contact and that they would eventually relent and change their minds, to let him join them in their tree house. He muttered at them, hoping they would feel threatened, threatening to go home to complain to his mother. That was his recourse, as he was desperate in wanting to join them. Unfortunately, the two were not moved.

Back then in the village, piped water was a luxury and only for the better-heeled. Wells were dug to ensure the constant supply of water to all the households within the vicinity. That village had two wells; one had a circular retaining wall, while the other was squarish in shape. The water from the circular one was not potable, as it was clearly dirty and muddy and was only good for washing. It was heavily tinged orange, especially after a downpour. The square well had crystal-clear water and was used for cooking and drinking. The latter was situated about twenty feet from the star fruit tree and had only about a two-foot-high retaining wall.

Dean was about three-and-a-half feet tall. Back-stepping without eyes at the back of your head is one dangerous adventure. Dean was asking for trouble, as he found out later. *Splash!* His tiny legs hit the wall, his knee buckled, and he fell backwards into the water. He was drowning!

The strange thing was, he thought he was dreaming. The little he could remember involved kicking the sides of the muddy walls of the well and surfacing once or twice.

His time was obviously not up yet. Providence was smiling at him, as help was at hand. Another cousin, a burly, tall guy by the name of Joe, who had just returned home and was about to preen his pet parrot, heard the splash. He asked the two ignorant fools, "Where is your brother?" They were none the wiser, as their preoccupation had the better of their time—plucking the star fruits, washing them, and then gorging on them nonchalantly.

Joe approached the well with the parrot, first intending to wash his pet parrot and second to check out the source of the splash. True to his suspicion Joe was shocked when he gazed inside the well and saw Dean's tiny hands raising as if asking for help. Joe then shouted at the top of his voice that Dean had fallen into the well and yelled for help, just in case. Being huge and tall, Joe was able to reach down without much effort and plucked Dean from the jaws of death.

The few things Dean could remember after being revived were that everybody was scurrying around like headless chickens, and his mother, who was preparing for the Chinese New Year, burned her cakes. His dad applied whatever little knowledge he had of CPR and was pumping the water out of his tiny body, so Dean survived.

The water from the drinking well was then deemed undrinkable, as it had been contaminated. Far from crystal clear, the water quality was murky, and it was suspected that this was the result of Dean kicking the sides of the mud wall, causing the degeneration. Everyone helped empty the well for new water streams to flow. It took a couple of days before the well was flowing up to the usual level.

That was the first momentous junction of Dean's life—a Godsend, pretty much beyond anyone's control, but that incident made a difference in his life.

Dean had three siblings, two brothers named Henry and Danny and one sister by the name of Venus. The favourite of the family was Venus. Being the two older siblings, Henry and Danny, who were five to six years older than the two younger siblings, preferred not to involve Dean and Venus in most of their activities, so by default, the two younger ones had no choice but to create fun together. As a result, Dean and Venus had a special relationship, which endures today. They had each other for company on most days, as the two older siblings were never home. They developed games and had great fun together. Rainy days were their favourite time. They would make paper boats, which they would launch onto the streaming rainwater in front of their house, with an umbrella in one hand and paper boats in the other. Rushing in and out of the rain, they soon found that the umbrella was no longer of any use, as they were soaked to the skin. Soon after their mother discovered their prank, their juvenile laughter turned to cries.

On yet another occasion, both Dean and Venus decided it was time for their mother to buy them new wooden sandals. In truth, their sandals did not need replacing; they were still usable. So in order to justify the purchase to their mother, they went to a lot of trouble looking for something to artificially wear down their sandals. They found a discarded concrete patch with very rough surfaces and decided that would be the ideal tool to achieve their objective. Both began their wayward shaving of the soles of their sandals by exerting them onto the rough concrete slab with as much pressure as possible. It was hard work, and they laboured with full concentration for hours. Of course they were caught by their mother again and were spanked.

Both had their fair share of quarrels, which could be expected, especially at a young age. The relationship between Dean and Venus was no different, and that strengthened the bond between them. Venus was as stubborn and defiant as Dean and so some kind of juvenile violence could be expected. One day they had a usual quarrel, and Dean was unhappy with her attitude and told her to keep quiet, but Venus challenged Dean to silence her. Dean landed his fist on her mouth, and blood streamed down her lips. This time Dean received the sharp end of the stick from their father for being a bully.

But soon after that the two kids were up to no good again at home.

Life at that time in the village was simple and fun. Dean's family was quite poor, but they never starved. Home-cooked meals were the best and his mother was very handy in the kitchen. She was very proud of her cooking and could whip up some really mouth-watering fare in no time.

His parents had a loose division of labour between them. His father would buy the fresh food items like fish, pork, and vegetables, while his mother would take care of buying the dried food items like onions, ginger, dried prawns, dried chillies, and flour. and of course the cooking. It was amazing how his parents coordinated their purchases. The fresh produce buyer would second guess what the chef would prefer to whip up as Dean was sure his father would purchase whatever he liked but not knowing how they would eventually turn out. But there was one thing Dean remembered that could possibly explain this unspoken arrangement between his parents. There were times his mother would fry all the fishes that his father had bought, and these were supposed to last a few days. These would be fried again and again. Other times his mother would cook a big pot of pork in black sauce that would last the week. The strange thing about that was Dean, his siblings, and his father never complained, as the overnight food was just as good.

His father would do the marketing on a weekly basis on a Sunday. Being a Roman Catholic, he would attend the 6.30 a.m. Mass every Sunday, lugging his favourite rattan basket. After the Mass he would proceed straight to the wet market for his weekly routine. Dean would occasionally accompany his dad, not to help, really, as he would be more of a nuisance, but to mingle with the crowd and soak in the fun. The market was located at the mouth of a small tributary where all the fishing boats were anchored.

After their catch, all the fishermen would dock and unload their catch, which would then be auctioned off. Many auctions happened simultaneously, and it was a wonder how transactions could ever take place. With the din that was created, Dean was certain there would be mistakes when money changed hands, but everyone seemed happy and satisfied with the deals. That market was the central distribution point for all the fishmongers who came from all over the vicinity to buy their stock for the day. Some had stalls at some smaller wet markets, while others would hawk their purchases on their bicycles around the villages.

Dean's mother would take care of buying the dried provisions from the shop in the neighbourhood. Dean's family could not afford a telephone to do the ordering of these dried stuffs. So poor Dean had to make a shopping list of what his mother wanted to order and then would either walk about or cycle the one kilometre to do the needful. Deliveries would be done the following day by the store's staff. Sometimes cash would be paid upon receipt of these deliveries while at other times these would be done on credit. Payment was usually made upon the next order or within a thirty-day period.

Dean's mother had to scrape through her little savings from his father's meagre income as a clerk with a small shipping company to put the children through school. His two brothers had the benefit of having tuition. It was his mother who insisted they had tuition, as it was quite fashionable at that time. It was very much a kind of status symbol, much akin to having maids as helpers in the home these days. Dean's brothers Henry and Danny had once or twice weekly tuition sessions on several subjects. It was more an opportunity for adventure than to really enrich their intellect. Unwittingly, their mother was bankrolling the tutors from their dad's hard-earned money, and the duo was none the wiser.

As Dean matured with age and progressively with time, he made a conscious effort never to be like his older siblings but to do things very differently. And from what he had experienced, witnessed, seen or learnt in his encounters to be of help to those who need it, to teach those who are eager to learn, to share his experiences generously, and to be as charitable as humanly possible.

During his primary school days, Dean did well only in the first two years when he was never denied the first and second positions in class. Thereafter, at best he would be positioned somewhere in the middle of the class for the rest of the six years during his compulsory primary education.

That he did quite well in the formative years in primary school got him into all the 'A' classes. From the six years in primary school he had the misfortune to have the same teacher by the name Gigi for three years, a fierce lady with an iron fist who was not very proud of being a teacher of the school. Now why did he form that conclusion? She married a rather well educated and prominent person who was quite a social luminary, and when they tied the knot, their wedding was featured in the local papers, complete with their wedding photo. The photo caption was that she was a "teacher of a school which was located near . . ." another which she saw fit to name, but not the school that she was teaching in. Why? If she were proud would she have done such a thing? Unthinkable, was his conclusion!

Dean was in Primary 3, the very first year with Gigi. He was a real prankster and was classed in the morning session. The same room would be taken by another class in the afternoon. Teachers' working desks were always positioned beside the blackboard in front of the class, facing the students. During dismissal, all had to line up in front of the class waiting for the bell to signal that school time was over. Dean and one of his classmates jostled for vantage position to be closer to the teacher's chair and would dust the chalk onto the teacher's chair. Not content with that mischief, they progressed to placing thumbtacks and wished the teacher in the afternoon a 'comfortable' seating experience. No complaint was ever lodged, so it was quite safe to assume the victim must have been quite alert, or that he had skin so thick the thumbtacks had no effect on his rear, otherwise the two pranksters would have been in trouble.

Another incident worthy of mention was at another occasion during a momentary absence of teacher Gigi. The same two boys were horsing around the classroom with paper planes with the inscription ITALY (meaning I Trust And Love You) written in full. It was a juvenile activity attempting to be topical for Connie Francis's hit song. It was just not their day when Gigi caught hold of one the planes. Both had the thrashing of their lives so they would remember this incident for a long time. Their knuckles were badly rapped. 'Executioner' Gigi's torture tool was the duster. With these bloody bruises both were still required to write some few thousand lines, something to the effect that they should never resort to mischief again. It was one painful experience, based on an action they did not think deserved such harshness. There was nothing good that the punitive measures could have achieved except to aggravate their already illegible handwriting. It is hoped the Ministry Of Education would wise up to this silly, misplaced, and totally useless form of punishment. If anything, only the stationers would be pleased.

Dean's primary school days were fraught with many accounts of things that he, on reflection, was not too proud of. In the early years he was a street fighter or a gangster in the making, in the strictest sense of the word. He chose to be the champion of the weak, a kind of Robin Hood. Always available for his friends and regardless whether his friends were in the right or in the wrong, he would readily assume his role as their champion.

There was one Thomas, who was physically frail and was therefore an obvious target for bullies. One day he approached Dean and complained that so and so pushed him. Specifics such as why and how did not matter. All he needed to know was, "Who is the guy? Point him out to me." Never mind the whys and the wherefores. Dean was at best a puny guy with a mighty crusader attitude, and that was all he had. Of course due diligence was in place. He sized up the guy to determine whether he could take him. This assessment, however, did not take long and more often than not he would just go for him. That poor bully did not know what hit him and why.

This bravado did not last very long. He was about ten years old when he took on one other boy who was about the same age with the same physique. Of course he was no match for Dean and had to eat humble pie by picking himself up from the ground and walking away after the match. This particular fellow had revenge in mind and actually took up weightlifting, and it was about four or five years later that he looked for Dean and asked for a rematch. Now Dean might be a fighter, but he wasn't an unthinking one. He fought to win, as he recalled his father's advice: never take on a fight when you know your chances of winning are slim. His opponent's weightlifting regime had given him some very noticeable muscles, and by then he was much taller than Dean, who chose to walk away and still managed to hold his head high, perhaps to fight another day. There was no reason to have that rematch. Even though there was a small crowd, as any thinking person should know what to do—discretion is the better part of valour. Dean met up with this chap not so long after that and learnt that he took up the job as the Chief Fire Officer with a large oil company and was doing well with a good family, a nice car, and a nice house in good neighbourhood. When they happened to meet, the past encounters remained in the past and cordiality prevailed, which should always be the case among friends.

It was during the years in Secondary School that he strongly bonded with a group of childhood friends from the Altar Boys Society. It was then the four brats chose to call themselves the Magnificent Four (M4). This platform caught the interest of several others who expressed keenness to join the group, so with the admission of two more eager members, the group changed its name to the Magnificent Four plus Two. To date only two members of the original group fell out. So the new name has been so amended to reflect the new number—M4. Dean initiated regular lunch meetings with three monthly intervals to stay in touch, as these members are in their senior years. But the camaraderie is still very strong. Each of these members actually looked forward to the lunches, with each taking turn to host.

Had it not been for the religious grounding of the Altar Boys Society, Dean's life could very well be vastly different, more so given the fact that he had this latent 'heroic' trait of championing the causes of others. It would not be unthinkable that he could well be active in the underworld.

Well, things turned out all right, and as Dean had made a commitment to himself that he must be different from his siblings or for that matter anyone in any set environment; in fact, he told himself he must always be better. No way would he allow his parents to slog to afford him tuition. Although he did not have the benefit of extra lessons, he did not do too badly as a student, so when he took his Primary School Leaving Examination (PSLE) very lightly, his pride and ego took its toll on him, which he would realize later. The result was that he was only good enough for Secondary 1 C. The better students would be given positions in Secondary 1 A or B. He took comfort that there were quite a few classes after C . . . up to E.

It was quite a culture shock for most students to find themselves in secondary school. The demands were quite beyond their imagination. It was drastic shift of mindset from the multiple-choice questions saga, when all the students needed to know then was to be acquainted with the alphabet and the numbers and to know where to position them in the correct brackets to writing as in Secondary School—and not just writing but a lot.

When in Secondary 1 C, Dean had this classmate seated just in front of him, one whose scrounging habit for snacks from others after recess knew no bounds. His incessant behaviour became very annoying. *Must teach him a lesson,* Dean told himself! Dean's insidious character got the better of him. He was nursing a cold, and on that fateful day he had a great abundance of phlegm to spare and boogers for added measure. As usual he bought some fat and meaty dried plums, this time not for himself. His very old pen knife, which was rusting heavily, was his scalpel. Using this knife he created a gaping dissection, big enough to contain his phlegm and booger without raising suspicion. Then he managed to recondition, a la cosmetic surgery technology, to the plum to seemingly appear untouched or even better and more tempting appearance, post operation. True to expectation, this scrounger asked for free titbits after the class break. The treated plum was then gladly presented to him and without so much as to look at what was offered he quickly stuffed it into his mouth, appearing to be enjoying himself thoroughly. Both Dean and his co-conspirator were worried that he would call in sick the following day. But he didn't. Phew!

The first term exam results for Secondary 1 was over. In class Secondary 1 C, the difference in the results between the top third student and the fourth was too stark for the school not to take notice. The interval was quite big, big enough for the top three students, Tim, Henry, and Dean, to be 'promoted' to Secondary 1 A—an exercise that was unheard of. A promotion within the same standard within the year was quite an achievement.

Suddenly in Secondary 1 A, Dean realized he was not a science student, and it was there that he realized his shortcoming. Compounding that, among the so-called brighter students, he experienced how selfishness was spelt. To be fair, there were some who were more than helpful than others. But not many were forthcoming. He struggled with all the science subjects. With regard to Physics, his favourite peeve was and still is the subject of density. How to calculate and so on was beyond him. That was when he realized that he was not A*Star material! Opting for Arts was obvious! But true to the school's meritocratic system, he was selected to Science stream for Secondary 3. Just days before school reopened after the long yearend holidays, he approached the school principal, Bro Albert, and said he would like to switch from Science to Arts. Of course he tried his best to dissuade Dean. He said there were students who had asked to be in Science stream although they did not qualify yet did not mind to be on the waiting list. Such was the high demand for the perceived status of Science class.

Without a doubt, the social status of Science students far outweighed the Arts. Sad to say for those who chose to hang on to this misconception as when the commercial reality after schooldays were over, it would be quite a different story. One would find out later on in life that aptitude and attitude would always prevail. It would never be whether one was a Science or an Arts student. This would never be cited as a criterion for job application. Of course it must be admitted that a decision to faithfully embrace Science as a subject would be applicable for those who would prefer to extend this love for Science-related disciplines like medicine or engineering, for example, through to their working lives.

It was unthinkable for a student who was selected to pursue studies in the snooty Science stream to downgrade, and to do so wilfully. But Dean was adamant and didn't care too much about such a status—not that he knew that it would not matter to his career choice later on in life. To be in his comfort zone and to do well in his studies took precedence. He had decided. Bro Albert asked whether his dad was aware of his decision. His answer was plain and simple. It was his life and his dad would not be able to take his exams nor lead his life for him. Even he was surprised that he had the gumption and audacity to do that as a fifteen-year-old. That was the first independent decision he made for himself that made a difference. He had learnt!

Another of Dean's experiences worthy of mention that set another platform for learning about human behaviour was when he was in Secondary 2 A. He had the misfortune to be seated in front of the brother of the Art teacher by the name of Dick. This classmate was also a prankster. It was Art lesson. Dean was playfully poked by something sharp and of course his reflex action was obvious, much to the annoyance of Dick. It was very disappointing that as a teacher, Dick was least interested in listening to Dean or to allow a hearing at least. It was his brother Dean was complaining about, so he would hear nothing of that, that his brother could be the culprit who made Dean yell. Instead of investigating the problem, he went straight for Dean, who had to suffer several knocks on the head with a chalk duster. Dean surmised that his reputation as a fighter must have done him in. The pain and embarrassment was quite something. On hindsight he wished he'd been able to stand up to the teacher. Whenever he recalled this incident, he often wondered what would have happened if he had proceeded to lodge a complaint to the Principal of the school or the Ministry Of Education. Would Dick have been warned, suspended, or dismissed? Well, one will never know. Years after, Dick decided to leave the teaching profession and venture into some business of his own by setting up a retail outlet for knickknacks, and of course Dean hoped his attitude would have changed for the better. This time he would have to deal with real people, not submissive students who would stand up to him and worse, may even sabotage him and his business. It was one unforgettable experience for Dean. Innocence punished! Blood is thicker than water. Reputation did not pay.

A note to all teachers—one must learn to take time to listen, especially to those who fall prey to pranks. A classroom environment is an extremely vulnerable and fertile ground for these. More so when siblings or blood relations are involved; impartiality and open-mindedness must prevail, lest favouritism shall be held suspect.

Regarding Dean's own academic pursuit, he had no regrets opting to go for Arts instead of Science stream. He did quite well in his 'O' Levels and was granted a position in Pre U 1 (Arts). Among his classmates were some Science students who did not quite make it at O levels. Their situation would have been quite different had they chosen the Arts route at the very beginning. It was a real pity.

Blissful Junction

Dean decided to join the local Roman Catholic Church's Altar Boys Society. All altar boys were involved in a lot of church activities by default and Dean was not complaining. There was this beautiful young girl with long flowing hair, spotless complexion, and the sweetest smile that melted his heart. She was with another church society and among the other activities, she was selling the church's weekly bulletins every Saturday afternoon before the Novena service. Such bulletins are now freely given away at all churches, but at that time each bulletin was priced at ten cents a piece.

Dean had seen her on many occasions, but he thought he should try to meet her up close, so he seized every opportunity to buy the bulletin from her and her only, ignoring the other peddlers. Many times he would deliberately and deviously use a one dollar note to buy one bulletin, compelling a change so that more time would be accorded him to spend with her as she would have to struggle and sometimes run around to look for loose change without realizing there was this secret admirer enjoying every moment of it.

There were times the Church society she belonged to had meetings held on the second level of the Parish building. Mischief got the better of Dean, and there he singled her out and blew kisses unabashedly within full view of all. He was never afraid or ashamed of what he did, as he had fallen head over heels in love. Totally!

But what was her name? So began the search and within the Altar Boys Society, one fellow altar boy by the name of Peh confidently told him the girl's name was Catherine and even volunteered to bring Dean to her home. And so they did. Together they cycled to St Gerard's Lane where Catherine lived. Peh then yelled out *Catherine!* at the top of his voice, hoping that showing up at her front door would catch her attention. It did not work, and luckily too, as it was the wrong person and of course the wrong house, as he found out much later. It would have been one big embarrassment.

It was the second day of Chinese New Year on 14 February, 1969, which happened to be Valentine's Day, when Dean was invited to attend a party at Melvin's house. He was never a party animal, but for some strange reasons he went.

It was the right decision and one that would totally change his life. Wham! There he met the girl of his dream that night. The girl he had been dreaming about. The girl he blew kisses to. The girl he bought the church bulletins from . . . . She came with a couple of friends, and he mustered the courage to ask her for a dance even though he was never a good dancer. That was the greatest moment of his life. It was then that he found out that her name wasn't Catherine, it was Bridget. He danced like never before (not that he'd had many before anyway), but it was the most delightful moment of his life. Heavenly! He never allowed her time off from that moment on to dance with anyone anymore. She was and would be his—a Godsend forever!

So smitten was he that he had to see her again. As it was still within the fifteen days of the Chinese New Year, he saw that as a good enough reason to pay Bridget a visit at her home. To do that and to visit her alone might not be the right thing to do at such an early stage of their relationship. So he got hold of another fellow altar boy, Kevin, for company, and both marched to Bridget's home, only to find her and Angie (Bridget's good friend) cycling from her home. They were apparently on their way to some other place. But upon seeing the two boys and learning from them that they were there to pay Bridget a visit, they were so thrilled as they got invited. Phew! They were in luck! Obviously Bridget and Angie had to amend their itinerary to accommodate the boys. They felt honoured. Both Bridget and Angie accompanied them all the way to her home. The visit was predestined.

"Somebody Loves You," a beautiful song by Skeeter Davis, was coincidentally playing on the radio at Bridget's home during the visit, and that song remained as one of Dean's favourite hits of all time. And his favourite line from the song was and still is, "That somebody is me." It was truly pre-destined!

Not long after that day, about one month later, they began seeing each other quite frequently. The intervals between visits grew shorter and shorter until one day they were meeting daily. Bridget was still doing her O levels, and Dean was just starting out in the commercial world selling Tadler typewriters, earning only $180 a month plus whatever commission he could earn, and that was all Dean was worth.

Their first date was watching a movie at Broadway at West Coast. The movie was titled *Brain Stealers* starring Lily Ho, a Chinese movie from Hong Kong. After the show they walked around window shopping at Tay Ban Guan, a small shopping centre. There Bridget was admiring a teddy bear, and Dean wanted her to have it although he could ill afford it. That was because he had about only $50 left in his pocket, which was to last him for the rest of the month, and the bear would set him back by $20 or so. Bridget declined. He was saved, otherwise he would most certainly have had to resort to borrowing from colleagues the next working day.

Bridget was taking typing classes at the church's Parish Hall for self-advancement. After her typing class Dean and Bridget would meet at a predetermined bus stop to board a service that would bring them through to Ponggol end, a journey that took about thirty minutes. The longer the distance and the slower the bus moved, the better. Upon reaching the terminal they would then take long walks for as long as their legs would carry them or as long as time allowed. Other days they would visit her home and talk and talk and talk. It was a very affordable courtship, as they did not have to spend any money at all. It was a good thing as Dean did not have much to spare.

It was on 12 January, 1974, a good five years after their courtship, when Bridget and Dean tied the knot at the Nativity Church, the place where he blew her many kisses, purchasing church bulletins from her, and the many Masses that he had served as an altar boy.

Maxi was their best man, Lilian their maid of honour. The church service was a simple affair. It was a one-hour Mass, and Dean's former form teacher, Bro Francis Toh, was the organist who played his rendition of "Showers of Blessings," which greeted the about-to-wed couple as they walked down the aisle.

True to the tradition of yesteryears, they then rushed to Brightway Photo Studio at Serangoon Road to have their wedding photos taken. That was very unlike today, when the wedding photo shoot would have been undertaken months before the actual day.

Dinner was at Princess Restaurant—a restaurant of some reckoning at that time. Never to burden his mother with money matters, Dean managed to save enough for the day's proceedings. It was quite a formal affair. Half the guests were in formal attire, mostly from Memory International, (MI) though relatives preferred the casual treatment.

Although tired from dinner, the new Mr and Mrs Dean had to catch some winks as they had to catch an early flight to Hong Kong to begin Dean's assignment as a guest instructor for a class of new MI hires.

And so began their honeymoon from Hong Kong to Taiwan, Korea, Japan, the Philippines, and Thailand. They had two great weeks of their lives.

On their first night at Lee Gardens Hotel in Hong Kong, he had a meeting with the Singapore boys, John and Bernard, and one Malaysian, Teddy Tan. Bridget and Dean had yet to even lie down on their honeymoon bed when Teddy beat them to it, christening it by lying spread-eagle and really enjoying himself. Until today Teddy lays claim that because of what he did, Dean now has three beautiful children. Maybe he was right!

One episode of their honeymoon was more memorable than the rest. It was in the Philippines. Dean's bravado and lack of experience in not having a prior reservation nearly did them in. Upon arriving in Manila, they tried booking their hotel at the airport. That they did without a hitch in the preceding countries gave them a false confidence, so they wrongly took for granted that it should be all right to assume the same for every country.

Lucky for the newlyweds Dean was working for MI, an international company, and that saved the day. The fraternal network helped. He called MI and asked for help. Without anywhere to go, Bridget and Dean lugged themselves all the way to MI's Philippines office while the colleagues at MI sought help, using whatever influence they had. True enough, before long they were able to check the honeymooning couple into The Filipinas, a nice five-star hotel.

A lesson that he had learnt was to never leave anything to chance. Better plan and book accommodations well in advance. Never leave creature comforts to chance, more so when you are with your loved ones.

Bridget has been Dean's wife for forty years, and with five years thrown in for their courtship, they have had forty-five years of blissful happiness. She has honoured him with three beautiful children, Charlotte, Donny, and Evangeline.

It was during the wedding dinner that one of Dean's classmates approached him, and after the usual pleasantries, whispered, "Shotgun, is it?" Dean was merely twenty-three years old, had barely worked for three years, and being one of if not the first in the class to get married, why the rush if not for some very compelling reason? So it was understandable why that thought crossed the former classmate's mind, never mind the tactlessness. Dean should not have been too sensitive to that remark or why was the classmate had been so presumptuous. Dean's impulsive response was, "You wait! I will not have children for at least two years." He might have been young, but there was no doubt about his maturity. He was and still is certain that Bridget was and still is the lady of his dreams, his soul mate for life and beyond.

Two years after their marriage, Bridget one day complained to Dean and to his mother-in-law that she had this strange indigestion feeling. Mom baked sea salt and rubbed it on Bridget's stomach, believing that the treatment would ease the pain. This did not happen. Mom then brought Bridget to a Chinese physician. It was then that they discovered Bridget was pregnant with Charlotte. This would fulfil Dean's prediction and commitment to his former classmate at the wedding dinner that it would be at least two years before he became a father.

Charlotte was one cheeky brat. First when Bridget was carrying her, she had swollen legs for almost the entire duration of the pregnancy. Charlotte was adamant in sitting up instead of behaving like most other foetuses in their mother's womb to lie facedown. Tried as he may, Dr Chan could not bring her around. Charlotte had to be delivered via caesarean because of this. Bridget underwent thirteen hours of labour before Charlotte could be brought out. When Dean first caught sight of Charlotte, as he similarly did for all the three children, he had to make sure each one had ten fingers, one nose, two ears, and ten toes. Then they must cry! Dean never saw Charlotte cry! That was worrisome. Bridget reassured Dean that Charlotte not only did cry, she yelled. That was good enough! Anxiety drifted away.

When Donny, Dean's second child, was on his way into the world, they chose Mount Alvernia for the delivery. There the nurse asked whether Dean would be keen to be in the delivery room to lend moral support to Bridget, to which he shamelessly declined. "Coward!" the nurse cried out loud, bent on shaming him in front of all the hospital staff. In fact, he had every intention of being in the room with Bridget but somehow the cowardice in him surfaced. He regretted missing out as Charlotte and Evangeline,

Dean's third child, came through caesarean, so he was denied witnessing deliveries of his kids by default, as all caesarean births are out of bounds for husbands. Dean would never bear witness to any delivery.

Bridget had the most difficult pregnancy with Evangeline. For almost eight of the nine months, she could not stand the sight or smell of food. Her reaction to rice was the worst. She would throw up. Instead of gaining weight, which was to be expected in any pregnancy, she was losing. Dean chose not to have lunch meetings with his clients as lunch hours were spent looking for all kinds of food, so she would at least have some kind of intake of nourishment. That she ate, Dean realized, was really to humour him and not to waste food that he had taken so much trouble to buy for her, and that was good enough. Dean was glad that she obliged, otherwise he would not dare speculate the likely outcome of the pregnancy. As with Charlotte, Evangeline was equally naughty and had to be delivered through caesarean section.

Somehow the two girls were more uncooperative than Donny.

After every birth, Dean's first thought was always Bridget's well-being, as it should be, rather than the newborn's. That was most important. In his mind it has always been that whom you did not know did not matter as much. It was who you knew and loved that mattered. It was a blessing that all three children had been delivered successfully.

The lesson that can be learnt from this blissful junction is never give up on anything you want. Perseverance is not good enough. Persistence is not good enough. The combination of courage and boldness is dynamite. That was what counted. You see, you go, and you conquer.

Yet another lesson is "Faint heart will never win fair lady." Always treasure your loved ones. They are a rare breed. Do not compromise on love. Give all. Share all.

Marriage and parenthood are serious commitments that have to be carefully thought through. Do not trivialize this momentous event with frivolity.

Fatherhood and Children's Academic Pursuit

The experience Dean had during his school days when he decided to switch from Science stream to Arts prepared him well for fatherhood. He consciously made it a point to never influence or to decide for all his children to do any course of *his* choice in their academic life. It must be their decision. The line he used for all three children was, "I will not be your excuse for failure in life," as we would have heard enough stories how some people had to pursue certain courses dictated by their parents, much to their regret later on in life, and for some to a lesser extent as they were able to readjust, but time would have been lost.

As his children were growing up and Dean had to confront the major issue of what course or discipline they should go for, he made a conscious effort never to compel them to go for anything they did not like. A general discussion on the pros and cons of each of the courses would precede the children's decision as they must be given the latitude to decide what would interest them not what would interest their parents. They must have the passion to embrace whatever they like so they would be able to excel.

Charlotte was contemplating on taking a course in the Environmental Design Faculty with a local institution, and the only one exception he made to this non-interference ruling was to tell her that the Fine Arts course may not be commercially viable in the context of a small market, especially in Singapore, and to opt for some others that would better prepare her for a more financially rewarding career. He told her to take a look at all the van Goghs of the world who would be rich and famous only after death. Of course that was a simplistic and narrow analysis, but he was glad he succeeded.

Charlotte opted for a Graphic Design course and qualified as an Interior Designer. She struck out on her own at a very young age and eventually decided to work as a Real Estate Agent and to make use of her Interior Design skill as value-add. She has no regrets. In fact, she has done well for herself. Today, Charlotte is happily connected to her soul mate.

Donny was and still is a Creative thoroughbred. Good thing he decided to take up a degree course in Creative Writing and earned himself a degree from America in the same discipline. In fact, music was his life, and he would very much have preferred to immerse in a music career. Unfortunately in manner like with Charlotte, Dean told him that in the local context, singing and music would not bring in the dough. Good thing he bought it too.

Donny's love for music probably had something to do with the singing contest he took part during his schools days with the song "Let It Be" and won.

His room was filled with musical instruments and related paraphernalia. For his girlfriend he would compose songs with meaningful lyrics and complete with his own vocals for that special added effect.

Donny used to have a band, and members were his ex schoolmates. He would spend all his leisure hours jamming and recording with his bunch. They took part in a local talent contest titled Come and Get it and managed to be in the finals. Pity they did not win.

After graduation he had a two-year stint as an Admin Executive with Apha Pte Ltd and had enough. He then chose the line of work closest to his heart—copywriting— and was doing well in a relatively large local ad agency. He then chose to switch to become Marketing Manager with a large local manufacturer of jewelleries and is enjoying himself. Donny is also happily connected to his newfound soul mate.

The youngest child, Evangeline, had a faint interest in becoming a doctor, but that disappeared as quickly as it came. Quite unlike her two older siblings, she was more business inclined and was quite accustomed to quick decision making. She spent six months in a college of her choice, one located at least fifteen kilometres from her home, and had to contend with daily sleep deprivation due to two-to-three-hour trips to and from school, hardly having any time to do anything else. After six months and barely one week to school for the second term, she woke up one day and suddenly decided to take the Polytechnic route.

Dean made a rather quick enquiry with Singapore Polytechnic and luckily for her there were vacancies in Business Management Faculty, which suited her well. She opted for Hospitality Management course and as she enjoyed the course she excelled.

It was four-and-a-half years since she joined a private commercial enterprise within seven days after graduation. She has not stopped complaining about the short break that she had as compared with the rest of her cohorts, who took time to travel and enjoyed themselves before launching into the corporate world. But she has not regretted it as within two years she was promoted to Admin Manager, a position she deserved. She had a couple of staff working under her.

Adventurous by nature, Evangeline had to sample almost every conceivable sporting activity, including bowling, swimming, badminton, golf, wakeboarding, and tennis but has yet to excel in any. As an example, in an effort to sample badminton she often missed hitting the shuttlecock at service. She was undaunted by the accompanying embarrassment of these frequent air shots but never allowed such things to dampen her spirit and resilience. She still claimed she can play the game.

Evangeline is now happily married and a mother of a beautiful daughter by the name of Karie Beth.

Friendship, Marriage, and Parenthood

At this point I'd like to touch on the subjects of friendship, marriage, and parenting. Dean and his wife, Bridget, made it categorically clear to all three children that race and religion would not matter in their choice of friends. And for those who wanted to extend that friendship into one more serious and enduring in nature, they must ensure that relationship maintained certain fundamentals. Dean and Bridget shared with them the must-haves: the parents must know who their friends are, their names, the jobs they held, where they lived, and their contact information for obvious reasons. One will never know when this information will come in handy.

Whenever he and Bridget touched on this subject with their children, they never failed to philosophise that when they meet that someone special, age difference should never be a factor. But take time to filter out and examine structural characters, like whether that person is caring, has integrity, and has the financial ability to see you through life.

There is also one other condition often cited by parents: you must never marry anyone other than someone of your own race or religion. This was one Dean did not quite fully agree with but understood that it had merits that might be worth thinking about. The caveat here is that for as long as both were aware of the pitfalls and took steps to avert a potentially explosive problem, it could be sorted out, although it was relatively more difficult and one, which requires a lot of understanding, tolerance, and patience.

Let us understand how this 'discriminating attitude' came about. In the parents' minds, marriage is a partnership for life. That seemed reasonable and made sense to have a couple, who would share the same culture, beliefs, and religion without the need to impose or compromise. This is borne out of the belief that couples should always try to spend time and to do things together, to be as likeminded as possible (not necessary to agree on everything but to respect each other), and share the same interests so that quality time can be spent together. Coming from different backgrounds, cultures, and religions, each would have very different practices and observances. It will be a pity if one wants to attend a religious function and the other could not or would not. That may possibly present itself as a latent catalyst for a problem (and sometimes an explosive one) in the future. Be careful here, as the adoption of 'separate' ways will play on the subconscious, leading to much regret. "Since you do not wish to partake in my function, why should I take part in yours", giving rise to an insidious crack. A tit-for-tat syndrome. A dangerous wedge is forming as the structure is weakening and collapse is imminent.

Never impose conditions on yourself. Never tell yourself that by a certain age or by a certain date you should marry, as you will never know when that special someone will appear before you. With a self-imposed deadline, there is a certain urgency that will serve to diminish the importance of the many criteria for a good marriage, and compromising the important traits for such a commitment is not good.

Overlook secondary and petty faults like slurping, sneezing loudly, snoring, grinding teeth while sleeping, and other small character traits. These are not important, and some can even possibly be corrected over time. In any partnership there will always be ups and downs. It is the necessary process which serves to strengthen the union. If all is hunky dory as are constant and frequent quarrels, all is definitely not well. As humans we have our failings, and in the course of a marriage of many years it is not possible that there will be no rough edges. If these do not present themselves it means there is a deliberate cover-up, so the relationship is built on pretences. This bottling up will explode one day. On the other hand, a muted response to the surfacing of such failings is also a prelude to an imminent problem, as it forms a fertile ground for a latent nuclear outbreak. That can also be interpreted as general apathy. Something is amiss. We cannot choose to ignore that. And if there are frequent quarrels, something is not quite right.

On the latter, Mitch Albom, author of *Tuesdays with Morrie*, propounded 'four precepts of a good marriage', which Dean fully subscribed to.

One: respect your spouse, for the lack of respect will only court problems and trouble. For a harmonious marriage, this must be the most important and essential component for the marriage to work.

Two: you must compromise, or there will be trouble. Again this hinges on the fact that nobody is perfect, so please allow some slack for your spouse, as much as we need for ourselves too.

Thirdly: be open in your communication with your spouse. If one cannot be open, communication problems will arise, as we will be guilty of dishonestly disregarding the issues, as if nothing is happening.

Fourthly: it is best that both share the common set of values as much as possible, failing which we would only be tilling the ground for seeds of dissent to germinate to the detriment of the marriage.

Dean told his daughters that one important fundamental is the partner's capacity to financially support the family: basic shelter, the food on the table, and the children's basic education, as financial matters are often a pivotal point as the cause of many families' break-ups. While dating, one's generosity or lack thereof can be quite telling.

Andrew Loh, one of Dean's dear friends who was well known for his candour, was extremely down to earth when he said, "If I were a girl, I would not mind marrying an ugly husband, as long as he can provide the necessities—and better still some luxuries—for me and my children. When I have to make love with him I shall close my eyes and pretend he is good looking or the likeness of some famous stars. After all it will be over in a matter of minutes, but I shall have a life that is worry-free". One can see the wisdom of his thinking.

The second fundamental is fidelity. This one is a lot trickier than the first. But sometimes situations can surface. For example, look at his integrity at the workplace. Is he on the take? Is he prepared to compromise his principles in the pursuit of career or money? Does he take care of his parents or siblings? Is he charitable?

Now on the subject of parenting. Parenthood is a lifelong responsibility. Bearing children is a moment's decision. Bringing them up to be socially responsible and able adults takes some serious thinking and is a long process. Financial ability to do so is so important.

Here are some thoughts on the vocation of marriage, before touching on the subject of parenthood.

We have often heard of the riddle that if a man's wife and mother were drowning and he could only save one, which one should he choose? This is a highly controversial matter, but the importance cannot be ignored. Many would argue that it is only right that one should save the mother; after all, in one's life time we have only one. Very politically correct. So it follows that we should let the wife drown. This is a real poser! Would that be the correct thing to do?

On Dean's wedding invitation card he imprinted on the cover a quote from the Bible, "What God has joined let not man put asunder". This is a very insightful quotation, one that seeks a deeper search into one's relationship with our parents and our spouses.

Biologically, one cannot choose who will parent us. This means we have become children of so and so by default; whether they are good or bad does not matter. Whether they had intended for us to see the world would be quite beyond us. Perhaps our procreation was never in their mind in the first place, in the midst of their conjugal moment. It is also possible that we are a function of a misbehaved sperm or a wanton laziness to adequately clothe ourselves in a moment of ecstasy. Granted mothers and fathers are God-sent, and we cannot do anything about that. It can be presumed that they should be responsible to take care of us and look after our welfare. In most instances this welfare attitude never ends, and we should be grateful. But that is not the point.

The difference between a parent and a spouse hinges on the important point of choice. When we choose our partner for life, it is a deliberate effort. We scour the earth to make a choice from among so many available candidates. Sure, we would have experienced some unrequited initiatives, and equally we would have belted some out with equal measures. Some frustrating encounters are a given. However, after some filtration we would have arrived at that one candidate who would have met most of the criteria that we have set. That one spouse will offer the psychological, financial, moral, and physical support of our causes in life. And the Gospel has endorsed, sanctioned, and decreed that this spouse and you are joined as one and shall never part.

It is therefore logical that the man should save his wife and leave the mother in God's hands. Dean fully subscribes to and supports this line of argument, agreeing this is a highly contentious issue with equal supporters and detractors.

Marriage is a vocation. It is a serious commitment to live through this decision. The next question is, how does one hold on to a marriage? It is indeed a challenge for any two persons to live with each other, warts and all, for up forty years—sometimes even fifty, sixty, or even seventy years. That would be more than a challenge. It is more a mystery how some couples do just that.

Dean has many friends who would readily testify to that fact that holding on to a marriage for more than ten years is daunting enough. In fact, many of his friends were divorced, and some even had more than one divorces.

Here we do not need to know how marriages fail, as many would be the first to let you know how to do just that. To fail in a marriage is as easy as ABC.

How to keep a marriage going is more difficult a task, so we shall dedicate ourselves to achieving this.

Dean was keen to learn the recipe of success of enduring and happy marriages. Some of these successful marriages were even match made. There was no courtship. So it became even more intriguing how these couples could endure the years together. The one possible answer is to examine the psyche of those couples who willingly agreed to arranged marriages and how they lasted. First, those who agreed to arranged marriages must, in general, be non-gregarious kinds, those who would prefer to be led than to lead. Ones who would feel uncomfortable making the first move. They would prefer not to attend any parties and are happy to be alone to do their own things. When compelled to attend such functions they would prefer to sit in a corner waiting to be introduced or waiting to be approached. When approached they would go red in the face straining to hide their embarrassment, unable and unwilling to make eye contact. Antisocial!

As such, it would be fair to say that these are the people who would most probably be more willing to make compromises for most things. It would not be unfair to assume that they would not go for looks and personality but everything else about the other person. It follows that the same could be said for the other. So there you are, two grown adults fully prepared to overlook a lot of the blemishes that come with the unknowns and armed with a great deal of respect, these couples could grow to like and accept each other over time.

Further, the time (and sometimes this can take many years) that normal couples would require for courtship to uncover each other's flaws would be the time these match-made couples take, post marriage, to know each other. So essentially it would be during their marriage that they would still be discovering each other, for what would have been a pre-marriage getting-to-know-you time for most. And with the passage of time it would be likely that each would grow to accept the other with compromises.

As they are very likely to be easy and amenable and not demanding, their post "purchase" dissonance would be in order. They would justify within themselves, that since they had each other "to have and to hold, till death do us part", and not to be a spoilt sport, they would learn to accept and tolerate each other till the end.

The social stigma that divorces would be frowned upon, especially for this group of sensitive people, would also evoke a more tolerant attitude. It boils down to managing expectation. Of course there will always be exceptions.

Another possibility and a rather unkind one is affordability. The consequence of a divorce can be expensive, and those who cannot afford to have one would rather resort to the silent response, preferring to grit their teeth to still live under the same roof and not communicate with each other. This would perhaps be another pseudo-successful marriage. To the outside world the marriage is working well.

Then there are those who typified the gregarious type and are able to hold on to their marriages. Dean knew a couple, Larry and Caroline, who after thirty years of marriage would still say they are very happy with each other. What is their secret? Although it is generally believed that both parties must actively work on their marriage, all Larry and Caroline required was for one to be active while the other was passive. In this case Larry was the active one who would choose to refresh the union every now and then.

Surprises lend themselves as yet another component worthy of mention to refresh one's marriage. This does not need to be expensive.

Before email and mobile phones became fashionable, communication between couples would be via fixed landline; that is, if both happened to have phones, otherwise it would be via letters (better still, love letters). With the proliferation of the mobile phone and email, letter writings became extinct. With personalized handwritten letters, there would be so much more one could write which at other time may not be pertinent to do so verbally. It is also more personal. Lines like "I love you" would be out of context and meaningless if uttered without feelings, more so when uttered daily, as it became a cliché. And there are those who could not for the life of them utter those words—preferring to label them mushy. But it is a whole new dimension altogether when it is done in writing. It is also very retro and therefore quite fashionable. So in order to relive those wonderful days, he chose to send home a handwritten love letter to Caroline to surprise her now and then. He would write things like it has been a long time since he last wrote and he had always wanted to write to express how happy he has been since Caroline became his wife. How grateful he was that Caroline bore them two beautiful children, how she must have suffered going through the pregnancies, and so forth. Caroline was thrilled. It was wonderful. It kept the romance alive. Unfortunately, this cannot be done too often as the novelty would wear out quite quickly.

In his daily morning routine in going to work, Larry would don his long-sleeve shirt and tie. That would be followed by a drive with Caroline for breakfast at a nearby coffee shop, after which Caroline would drop Larry at his office. She would then take the car for her own use. Once to surprise Caroline, Larry applied for leave without his wife's knowledge. On that morning, he would go through his usual daily routine like dressing up, but immediately after breakfast Larry would ask Caroline where they should head to spend the day together. It was then that Caroline realized that Larry was on leave. Caroline was pleased. They had the whole day to themselves, shopping, driving around the city visiting places that they had often mentioned that they should explore before, going to the movies, or just plain sitting down at a coffee house to spend quality time together. It was a little surprise that would serve to strengthen the bond and it did not cost much.

Larry made it a point to celebrate their wedding anniversary every year. On their twenty-sixth he decided to do something special. He called a florist and arranged to make the anniversary more meaningful. Since Larry and Caroline had twenty six wonderful years together he decided to compose thoughts using each of the letters of the alphabet on twenty-six different pieces of paper. He arranged with the florist to attach each of these twenty-six pieces with the appropriate line to each of the twenty-six stems of roses. The poor florist had to deliver in sequence, each stalk at a time, to Caroline with five minute intervals, to the pleasant surprise of his wife and family members.

Those were but some of the ideas Dean managed to draw out from his friends. But with a bit more thinking, ingenuity, and creativity one would be able to surprise one's spouse to add that sparkle to the marriage.

Now on the subject of parenthood. Having children is the culmination of a marriage. The joys of parenthood is immeasurable and one which should not be taken lightly. Care and profound thinking must also be accorded, since this parenthood journey should not be an imposition on others, like your own relatives, especially one's own ageing parents. It follows therefore that looking after one's children is one's own responsibility, and a heavy one at that. One's financial well-being is critical, the mental preparedness to share the responsibility of parenthood between the partners being another.

The most important philosophy all parents ought to share with their children very early in their growing up years and even more importantly as a pre-emptive measure is *not to be 'default nannies'* for your grandchildren. As grandparents, when you decide you have the time and the energy and would love to enjoy the grandchildren, then call for them, but never to look after the young rascals by default.

One story that is worth retelling to support this sentiment is about a son who preferred to continue living with his parents after his marriage. That initially was the good intention as the old folks were progressing in years and the son with his wife would provide welcome company for the lonely, ageing couple. Soon, the daughter-in-law was in a family way, and the old folks could not think of anything better than to offer themselves to look after the grandchild after he was born. The happiness of grandparenthood was overwhelming. Engaging outside help would pose a financial strain on the family. The influence of a maid may not be in the best interest of the young kid. After all, the grandson is flesh and blood.

Infant's laughter, even cries and the endless inquisitive questions with energy-sapping runarounds will be music to the ears and will never be an irritation. Mistake!

The grandparents were retired and had a good nest egg for which they had intended to make use of for a two-week holiday in China. They discussed this plan with the son, who in turn had a chat with the wife. The young couple then pleaded with the old folks to delay their planned holiday as both he and the wife had important projects that required them to be around the office and would not be able to take leave to look after their *own* son. The coincidence of the dates in question was uncanny. Only the young couple knew the truth. They would say things like, "We cannot take leave as we are needed to be in the office, otherwise our future would also be at stake". They were young and had to make a mark in the commercial world. They had to contend with office politics, whereas the old folks need not even have to work, let alone politick. The young couple was also right, so whose needs are more important, the old folks' or the young ones'?

Yet another story is about another elderly couple. After marriage, their son preferred to stay out on his own, away from his parents. But it became quite a different matter when his wife gave birth to a lovely boy upon the urging by the parents, who could not contain their eagerness to grandparenthood. Of course it followed the grandparents predictably offered to help look after the kid. It started with morning drop-offs and evening pick-ups on a daily basis and soon this practice of drop-offs and pick-ups were progressively reduced to once in a few days and then to once in a few months and now for 365 days there were no more pick-ups. The young couple now only visited their kids at the grandparents' home without bringing their own kid home anymore. Then came the second kid and the same saga repeated. Whose kids are these anyway? Now the grandparents had their hands full. Can you imagine this happening during your twilight years, when the body energy is fast depleting? Conversely, they had to rise to the challenge of energy-sapping sprints around the house and the frequent need to quell incessant juvenile outbursts and to be constantly alert so the grandkids would not be in harm's way. These can literally take their breath away, so much so that such an undertaking would make sleeping pills redundant. God forbid that these could also lead to a possible unmentionable outcome. It was even more heartbreaking for the old folks to find out later that the young couple took leave from their office and had their own holidays enjoying themselves without the old folks, and without their own kids, preferring not to even inform the parents. One could guess they did that with the sincerest intention not to cause problems and they must have also subscribed to the thinking that : The mitigation for not informing, even wilfully is not lying.

Therein lies the cracker. Do the old folks need to apply leave to enjoy their twilight years? To top it all, they would be required to apply their leave with no less their own child. Worse still, the application was rejected before submission. What is the world coming to?

Better avoid this pitfall, as it has this imminent prospect of degenerating into something quite catastrophic to one's regret.

The Difficult, Joyful, and Learning Years

Dean's cousin Kenny once worked for a petroleum company and had such a bad time with his boss that there were times Dean could see and empathise with his pain. Mild-mannered and never known to temperamental outbursts, but just to vent his frustration, Kenny once punched the wooden wall of a hut so hard that it cracked. That day must have been one bad day for him.

After a couple of torturous years, he called it quits and joined an American outfit as a sales representative for some freshly introduced products into Singapore. It was noticeably better outfit for him as he was almost always cheerful. It was telling that he enjoyed his work tremendously. He would go on and on about the many sales contracts that he had secured and the impending commission that was due to him by month's end. He did well to afford a good secondhand car as he climbed up the corporate ladder. He would take Dean for joy rides and to the movies. Kenny was Dean's role model. Dean often told himself that when he grew up he wanted to be like Kenny. He influenced Dean's choice to pursue a career in sales as he was impressed by his tenacity and perseverance in the face of an unkind manager in the petroleum company.

After his O levels, Dean spent one year in what was then called Pre-University in the Arts Stream, dreaming that perhaps one day he would be able to achieve a much-cherished childhood aspiration of becoming a lawyer. Unfortunately, that was not to be, as financial reality began creeping in. His father retired at fifty-five and was drained of his meagre pension leftovers that were quickly depleted to settle debts.

Prompted by their impatient call to parenthood, both of Dean's older brothers got married at twenty-one and moved out to fend for themselves. So there were his parents, his sister, and Dean, who were left to look after themselves. His sister was not working, and that put a tremendous strain on the little savings his parents put aside through the years.

Confronted with this realization, Dean had no choice but to quickly scour through the classifieds in the local newspaper for any job that would not discriminate against a youngster trying to eke out a living as a sole breadwinner for a family of four adults and was still in school. Furthering his education was then furthest from his mind. Survival of the remaining family members was key.

Of course he had many rejections. But he did reject some too. First Life Insurance and then *Encyclopaedia Americana* accepted him. He turned them down, as these did not have a basic salary, so he would not be able to help out in the financial well-being of the family. He had to have some basic take-home money, so he continued with his search for work with any organization which would meet and understand his needs.

Interviews after interviews yielded nothing. No job offers! It was a frustrating episode in his life. Luckily for him, after a long run, Mill & Phops, a large trading house, called him for an interview as a sales representative position selling Tadler typewriters. Not bad. The job name as sales representative, not salesman, was appealing. But alas, it was not to be. The divisional manager, Mr Mark Yeo, did not find him suitable. In his quiet analysis Dean came to realize it was a misjudgment on his part to have attended an interview for a job in his school uniform! The mere sight of a student must have been enough to put any interviewer off. Silly move.

Then came a letter from Supplies Corp on Owen Road asking him to attend yet another interview also as a sales representative, selling industrial glue to the timber industry. Upon arriving at the office he was ushered to a room to be interviewed by none other than Mr Mark Yeo from Mill & Phops—the guy who had turned down the school-uniformed candidate. He was there helping out the owner of Supplies Corp to select good candidates for the company. They were good friends, and Mr Yeo had the respect that was accorded him. During the interview, Mr Yeo, upon recognizing Dean, was more than sympathetic. In fact, Dean thought he took pity on him. He realized how desperate Dean was to look for work to heal the family's financial predicament, as he would have recalled during the first interview with him. Mr Yeo then told Dean to see him at Mill & Phops the following week, obviously knowing that in the timber business Dean would be swallowed up and would not last even one week.

It was in October 1968 when he was supposed to be sitting for the final exams for the first year in Pre-U when Dean started work selling Tadler typewriters, drawing a "huge" base salary of $180 plus $75 transport allowance. To supplement the family's finance he would give the entire $180 to his mother. He felt the conscious financial deprivation was the greatest motivation to spur him on to work doubly hard and to earn for his own basic survival from whatever variable commission he could get. And with the $75, he should be able to make do.

Cousin Kenny was so kind to give him the necessary working attire, a couple of hand-me-down short-sleeve shirts and ties. He would have to make do with those until he was able to afford more. It was then he realized that his puny body with short sleeves and a tie would not help him project a professional image. At best he would appear as a well-dressed delivery or messenger boy. It was then that he started to groom himself well as he began to appreciate how appearance would make a difference. He was able to do that after having received his first salary. It was long sleeves all the way after that.

With Mill & Phops, the daily routine was to drill everyone on the finer points of Tadler, being part of Tangrug, and that the typical high-quality German technology was well known for, etc . . . . The demonstration would require all the sales representatives to show off the high-quality stainless steel-type bars of the typewriters by chipping at coins. Dean wondered how the authorities would have reacted if ever they found out how the nation's coins were being mutilated, but one would have thought that for an unknown brand it was quite clever to adopt an unconventional method to sell. The price to pay, if ever it should come to pass, was worth it. Hey, that tactic sure worked and was impressive enough to sell, and the company did quite well.

Within three years as a scrawny youth, Dean made it to acting supervisor with Mill and Phops. There was one occasion that etched indelibly in his mind till today since selling Tadler typewriters.

An enquiry from Oily Exploration was given to him to handle. The address was somewhere on Grange Road. He did not know how to drive, much less own a car. Too poor to even dream of learning how to drive and too young to even go for driving lessons, his only form of transport was public transport—the bus. Taxi was a no-no, as the fares were not reimbursable. So he was left with one option— take the bus with the huge typewriter and the briefcase in hand and then stop somewhere along Grange Road and walk the distance—however long—to Oily Exploration, wherever it was. During the bus journey he did not manage to get a seat. The damn fellow commuters avoided eye contact, preferring to blind themselves to his plight. During that era, bus drivers were kamikaze wannabes, and sudden jerks and stops were common experiences and accepted as norm. Can you imagine the stand-up comedic performance he must have provided gratis for all the selfish fellow bus commuters with his balancing act? It was one memorable experience for him.

Finally the bus stopped at what is now Orchard Cineleisure, and Oily Exploration was perhaps two to three kilometres away. Of course Dean was none the wiser. So he had to walk along Grange Road with the typewriter and briefcase in hand under the scorching afternoon sun. Midway through the big walk, a car pulled up beside him and asked where he was going. It was Tony Tan, Sony Wong, and Henry Too, who were together in the car. It was on that fateful day that Dean met one great benefactor. It was Tony who took pity on Dean and gave him a lift in his car to Oily Exploration, that saved Dean a great deal of walking. As such Dean felt indebted to Tony for that kind act.

Tony and his friends were then working for Maxy, the agent for Boom calculators. At that time electronic calculators were the rave, and Boom was the market leader. They had a ball of a time, and there was Dean slogging away, peddling a relatively unknown brand of typewriter and exploring the geography of Grange Road. Dean was glad as that episode sealed a bonding friendship with Tony.

If there was one company that really brought out the best in everyone, it was Memory International (MI). Dean was a rookie and was one of a handful who was fortunate to be recruited despite his lack of a university degree.

So in order to qualify to join the ranks of MI, he had to undergo quite a few sessions before being offered a job. First there was this exercise, which he suspected had something to do with some suitability test or IQ test. All the selected candidates were seated in what looked like a classroom and were given test papers. After a week or so he was then informed that he should meet with the human resources manager, Eddy Tan and the field sales manager, Larry Chen . . . then to see Philip Thomas, who was then the country manager of office products. After that he had to see Tim Broadley, the MI country head who would have the final say on who would be employed.

It was during the interview with Eddy and Larry that Dean was shocked at being told by them, "Sell me anything." He could not believe his ears.

Sell what? Looking around the room and searching for a typically comfortable product for Dean to sell, both Eddy and Larry then prompted him to sell them his Bic ballpoint pen, which he had in his pocket. How? He was not prepared. Never mind; the daring in him told him to try. It was the best-selling spiel of his life, and it was the impromptu "sell" that got him the job.

Another candidate with whom Dean got acquainted with asked him for pointers that happened during the interview so he could better prepare himself, as his interview was scheduled the day after. Dean told him exactly what to do, but it was believed he was too well prepared and too slick for the interviewers to accept. He did not get the job.

One other candidate, Francis, was rejected after the interview with Philip Thomas. He was so distraught, and being the true blue salesperson he was, he penned a letter to Philip asking where he had gone wrong, as he would like to improve himself during his next opportunity with any prospective employer. Dean was told by him that Philip was so impressed by his sincerity that he was offered the job.

The new MI employees were destined for America for Basic School. They were also told there would be a competition among all the new MI employees. The corporate pride of MI Singapore would not be compromised. They must take home some cherished awards. There were no two ways about that. Altogether there were four who were employed. The other three could join quite quickly after tendering their resignations from their respective companies, but poor Dean had to serve the full notice period of three months. A pre-training programme was planned for all four in preparation for an overseas training stint! That was how serious the management viewed these pre-training sessions that in order to accommodate Dean these were conducted after office hours. The trainees had to sacrifice their social hours to do just that. Training to bring honour to MI Singapore sank in quite quickly.

The first lesson in grooming was harshly delivered. During one of the sessions, all were candidly told that they were required to only wear white long-sleeve shirts and dark pants, preferably black. Remember the training was done after office hours, so Dean took for granted that it would be acceptable to appear casual. He rolled up his long sleeves only to be told off by one of the seniors, "If you want to wear long sleeves, it must remain long sleeves, and if you prefer short sleeves, then wear one. Please do not have in-betweens."

It was at MI that Dean had quite a few firsts in his life. MI paid for the application for Dean's passport and all had advance cash to buy winter clothes as they were America bound during February for Basic School. That afforded Dean his first taste of flying, first taste of winter and snow, first taste of bowling, and the first taste riding a train. They were experiences of a lifetime.

At the Basic School in America there were altogether twelve new MI employees: four from Singapore, four from Indonesia, two from Philippines, one from Hong Kong, and one from Korea. They were put through some selling lessons from two instructors specially despatched from some other US office to walk all through before they could begin selling MI products. There were several products that needed to be explained. Recognition was given for the best demonstration for each of the products, and the overall best student prize were up for grabs.

The four Singaporeans worked very hard. They drilled themselves silly every night, checking and correcting each other. On the day of reckoning, three of the four took home the individual prizes. Dean was lucky to be awarded one of these and the overall best student as well.

The following year, 1973, the same four were bound for Hong Kong for Advance School. Again they had trainers from the United States, Hong Kong, and the Philippines as tutors. Prizes were again awarded, and Dean was again lucky enough to obtain one.

In 1974, Dean was told he was selected to be a Guest Instructor for a new school of new MI hires for Basic Sales school in Hong Kong. That coincided with his honeymoon.

His wedding was on January 12, and it was a wonderful coincidence that he had to be in Hong Kong on January 13 to begin the class. What a Godsend! Of course he was able to marry his honeymoon itinerary with the training. Bridget brought him all the luck. Their honeymoon was subsidized; what more could they ask for?

During the course of Dean's work at MI, he could recall one incident very clearly that even surprised himself. Demo machines were available for all to use. There was no real roster, but arrangements were made amongst colleagues so no one would be deprived. Dean had a few units with him, and it so happened that those were required by colleagues, which meant he had to organize their return. One morning he had the help of one office assistant, a strong, submissive and easygoing guy, to unload these from his car, which was parked in the building, using a custom-made trolley. In the building were four elevators for tenant use and one for service. While Dean and his helper were waiting for the elevator, a group of well-dressed and formally attired Caucasians alighted from their chauffeur-driven cars, who then proceeded to wait alongside both of them. When the elevator door opened, the helper pushed the trolley into the elevator guided by Dean.

One Caucasian man rushed out and while holding onto one side of the trolley he pulled it out of the elevator, with the helper in tow exclaiming, "This should be out of here to the service elevator."

Both were shocked, and it was then that Dean decided to do something. It was his turn to perform the exact opposite. He pulled it back inside, saying, "No, it's not. It is staying right inside here."

The man then exclaimed, "I am the landlord."

Dean replied, "So? I am from MI. If you are not happy about this, please speak to my boss. Do you want his telephone number?"

His white face turned red hot, and it was not from sunburn.

Dean had to do something quickly after the encounter. He sought out his boss and duly briefed him about what had happened.

His boss Gilbert Hum said, "Don't worry, some people ought to be put in their places." Such was the unquestioning support that the boss rendered. Would you not do anything for him?

It was sometime later that Dean found out this Caucasian man was indeed a senior person freshly imported from Hong Kong, when during the pre-1997 period, the colour of his skin would have made a difference there. Having grown accustomed to the haughtiness, he apparently thought he could get away with the same behaviour in Singapore.

Dean waited for the complaint to come in. It never did. Dean would have duly complied had the Caucasian handled the elevator situation in a gentler manner.

One of the most respected managers was Larry Chen, whose cheerful demeanour and characteristic laughter were his trademarks. He never had any nasty thing to say about anything or anybody. Here was a manager who would readily extend a helping hand to anyone in need. All who worked under him benefited a great deal. All soaked in as much as he would give. He was a great motivator.

Dean remembered this manager at MI—Gilbert Hum, who had a small frame even by Asian standards and a legendary determination and ambition. He would stop at nothing to achieve his goal. His personality was "taller" than his physical frame. He had presence. From a humble teaching background he became a salesman of Office Products (OP). He had record sales for a couple of successive years and as such was promoted to managerial level, with a group of salespeople under him. He was a no-nonsense kind of a guy, very used to hard work, well-spoken, and very bright. He achieved within two years what others took ten years. Even his sales performance as a manager was recognized in the region and was repeatedly hailed as an example of an excellent performer with great potential.

Soon enough he was made country manager of OP division. There was no doubt he was a highly ambitious man, and it was no secret he was after the top job. To better prepare himself, since he was not a graduate, he took an accelerated programme allowing him to take his master's degree all in one go. He made the grade.

OP division accounted for only a small percentage of the company's total performance. Data Products (DP) division had the lion's share of the total revenue and understandably the accompanying glamour that came with it. All the MDs (managing directors) in MI were from DP. So it was no secret that if anyone were to aspire to take over the MD position, he had better be in DP.

It came as a surprise (and paradoxically no surprise) that one day this Gilbert Hum, the OP Country Manager, decided to switch to DP as a sales representative. What? A sales rep? That was like a demotion, but that did not bother or deter him, although that was the question in everybody's mind and for good reason. To top it all off, he had to move out of the much-revered and envied status of a private office to be stationed in the general office, seated amongst everybody, sans privacy. In other words, he was among the "cattle class." He was just one of the boys. But he had a good reason for the move. He knew what he was doing. As expected, he did well again in DP and within a couple of years was made Country Manager of DP and within 5 years he rose to become among the first locals as MI's Managing Director.

There were a couple of lessons Dean learnt at this junction. Dean knew the reputation of MI and the social image that accompanied it. He heard and read about how admired the company was and the quality of the products and the quality of the people they hired. To be counted amongst such staff members would have been an achievement in itself. Never look down on yourself. He knew that as, he was very much aware that MI would never hire anyone without a degree, and he did not have one. So he went for it fearlessly and never felt intimidated and got what he wanted.

The spontaneous "selling" of the Bic ballpoint pen to Eddy and Larry during the first interview awakened in Dean the realization that to think on one's feet had tremendous advantages. To speak off the cuff was something he had never realized he could do. Sometimes it took a little event or an occasion to manifest some undiscovered and latent ability within us, which may otherwise remain dormant. He was grateful for the opportunity.

The other lesson that can be gleaned from failed candidate Francis's experience was not to surrender to circumstances too easily. Francis was sincere in wanting to know how he had failed in the selection process and sought feedback, and consequently he was successful in getting himself hired.

The "Caucasian encounter" taught Dean to never back down from bullies. Fight when confronted with unreasonableness. His "street fighter" persona got the better of him. He would have willingly retreated to use the service elevator had he not encountered impoliteness and brashness.

The one important lesson was the cheerfulness, the helpfulness, and the willingness to go the extra mile by this manager by the name of Gilbert Hum who implicitly imparted to all at MI through sheer examples to take care of those under his charge.

Be focused on what you want to attain in a company and work towards it. The example of this manager switching to become a sales representative of the division that mattered really taught Dean a great deal. He chose the breeding ground of the mighty by downgrading from a managerial position so as to stand a fighting chance to become the chief one day paid off.

Seventh Junction—the Good, the Bad, and the Ugly

Dean started working in 1969 and has not looked back since. He had many good mentors, many of whom he fondly remembered, as he had benefited a great deal from them. Equally there were some unmentionables.

From the crossroads Dean met with loads of people that afforded him the opportunity to discern the definition of "good" managers. The operative word here is "good," which should be defined correctly. One group taught people how to *REALLY* manage people well, how to motivate people, and even more importantly how to respect the individual, while the other taught *HOW NOT TO BE LIKE THEM*. So in essence, both offered great learning experiences.

Dean credited MI for having propagated the slogan "*Respect* the Individual." This encompassed the all-embracing concept of according human dignity to all staff members, as all are humans after all and should be entitled to some respect. They further fine-tuned this to an open-door policy, which they had truly carried out to the letter.

As a young man and in desperate need to earn a living for the family, Dean tried very hard to secure a job to support the family, as the sole breadwinner, totally oblivious to the fact that he was to be called up for National Service (NS). Undaunted, he worked his guts out, and when the enlistment letter finally arrived he was devastated. A full-time NS man during that time would take home $90 a month. He had his aging parents, his sister, and himself to look after, and that would never be enough.

He was really downtrodden not knowing what to do. In any case he was obliged to inform his manager, Mr Yeo, the date of the enlistment and also took the opportunity to unload his sob story to him and asked him to help him obtain a deferment. Mr Yeo, to whom Dean was totally indebted, not only empathized with his plight, he ferried him in his own car to the Ministry Of Defence to appeal on his behalf to amend his enlistment from full time to part time National Service, so that he could continue to work for him. The officer in charge was sympathetic and almost immediately changed Dean's status to part-time service so Dean could continue working.

Had it not been for Mr Yeo's intervention on humanitarian grounds, Dean's life would have been quite different. It was this same Mr Yeo that taught Dean that there was nothing wrong with rote learning. In his company, the daily routine would be to go through a demonstration of several models they were selling. Each of the salespeople would take turns. There was one colleague that could not even remember the lines taught. Every time he stood up he would be dumbfounded, petrified to the hilt, and would just gave his colleagues cold, hard, blank looks and then when he tried to speak, he was missing the lines and sometimes mixing up the sequence of the demonstration. It was a trying moment for all. But Mr Yeo was very patient. True to his belief, very soon this colleague would be able to rattle away without missing so much as a word and was mighty impressive at that. It turned out later that he was able to do so well and progressed to run his own business.

It was here too that Dean developed a sales management system that stood well for him in years to come. Each one would be given a geographical territory, and he devised a system to log in all the names of companies in such and such a street, the business they were in, the contact details, the person in charge, and any other information that would be meaningful and helpful to be able to sell better.

Another lesson he had learnt, and one he reminded himself very often never to fall into, was to not be personal in managing people and that to have as many hand-holding on-the-job training sessions with those under your charge. This is especially important for those who are new and needed this for confidence building. This time, it was how not to be like him.

This manager, a Mr Lim, was perpetually late arriving at the office. He frequently complained about his hangover and would slump his head over his folded arms across the desktop to rest. He was a rather big man who was a chain smoker and would be seen daily with a cigarette in hand. He would ask all whether there was anything he needed to know or any issues that needed to be discussed with him. That was it, the daily meeting, over in five minutes at best.

He would then go into a long litany about his night out with so and so and what they did and so on. Following that, he would just go out on his own. Rarely if ever would anyone go out with him. There was never an occasion when he would handhold anyone and show the ropes. There was no training. It was self-training all the way. The only training his sales people ever had was to read and learn from the instruction manuals that the manufacturers sent and sometimes ask the technical people for tips. So, on many occasions Dean had to bring home the equipment to learn how to operate and sell—on his own. The limit to this method was obvious, but the company had the great fortune to benefit from the strength of the brand, Boom, which sold itself. But the flipside was that all the salespeople learnt the hard way how to be independent and resourceful.

Salary adjustments were done on an annual basis. In one particular year, Dean's adjustment was a paltry $50, when his less-industrious colleague was given a lot more. That was when he learnt another lesson, to network even with colleagues. That had great benefits. It was through this network he was able to find out the disparity of the salary adjustment. The reason for his pitiable increment was that he was still single, whereas the other was married and therefore he needed more money to look after his family. That was Mr Lim's criterion for salary increase. Performance was never a consideration. So whether you worked hard or whether you bring in the business was not important to be recognized. But one's marital status was. What kind of philosophy was that? It was a period not worth remembering. To all aspiring managers, please take a cue to never inflict such neglect onto your staff. Treasure them, guide them, and help them, as they are the stanchions of the company.

Training and preparing and arming your staff with the necessary skills to do the job assigned are of utmost importance. This other company that Dean worked with, MI would "invest in," not "spend" money in training the staff. In fact, they had a whole department just looking after training. That made the philosophical difference in the approach to training. Everything was structured and planned. Without exception, everyone underwent some form of training; it did not matter which department or position one was in.

The approach was simple and straightforward. First, all new hires would be sent to be formally trained in a classroom environment, in a captive residential sort of way. In that manner all would be focused, no distraction, just training. Only after you have undergone this would you then be put on quota—in other words, you are then qualified to sell and earn your commission. That was for the first year and then the second and subsequent years and in between as well. Training was an ongoing exercise, regardless of whether it was in-house or outsourced. In fact, so liberal was this company that on one's own accord you could choose courses that you would like to take, and more often than not, such applications were approved without question. That was done way before a skills-development fund was ever conceived.

At some interval the boss would schedule a training round to gauge everyone's selling skills and then do what was termed as a "kerb-side conference"—a term used to describe a casual feedback session immediately after each sales call, where the boss would share his observation on what was well done and what could be improved upon. What a refreshing difference compared to the company before.

It was here at MI that all would be taught other skills, where Dean felt honoured to be among the staff members. Proposals and quotation were integral parts of the holistic selling function, but he was none the wiser. Asking his previous bosses to write proposals when required was part and parcel of his initiation to commercial life when he was just starting out. But that got stuck in his mind as the norm, mistakenly so as he found out later.

After a call when a prospective client asked for a proposal to be sent for their consideration he immediately fell back to what he had thought to be the norm. His boss in his previous company would write the proposal and Dean would do the necessary follow up. Upon returning to the office he left it at that, thinking his boss would do the needful. After a day's lapse he asked his boss where the proposal was that he was supposed to have sent. He was appalled! He would say, rather professionally but nonetheless purposefully, "It is your client, so it is your duty to do all that is required, including writing a proposal and seeing through the sale"

What? But he had never done that before. "My God, how am I going to do this?" crossed his mind. He was thrown into the deep end not knowing what next step to take.

Panic struck, and he was compelled to do some real work. Better do some research and seek colleagues' advice as to how he should write the proposal. One kind soul led him to a box file of past letters. Leafing through and reading them gave him some ideas as to the approach. The one distinct benefit of reading letters others had written was that you would feel the challenge to write better, more succinctly, and more appealingly. Finally he began his first-ever draft, writing whatever he could, and to be on the safe side he asked fellow colleagues' opinion and then finally showed it to his boss for approval before dispatching it. Since then he managed to stay afloat.

Recognition for one's performance is one great motivational tool, which was normal and expected at MI. Being recognized for doing a good job and being rewarded for it gives one a real high, more so when you are pitted against the region's staff and these sessions were carried out with much fanfare at a regional site in front of a huge crowd.

Being able to speak confidently is a definite plus, especially when you are in business. Somehow you will be able to get prospective clients to listen. Coupled this with a sense of logic and reasoning would make a good salesperson. This company not only groomed you but would also give staff opportunities to speak so that one will get acquainted and accustomed to excel.

In SuperNova Company, Dean's first boss, Mr Kim, was a great motivational teacher. He was so energetic that one could not help but be infected with his energy level. Everybody was evidently motivated as and when he spoke.

As a result we moved very fast and got things done at lightning speed, but never impetuously. He was always there to guide and help. He would not fight shy if he had to make nasty decisions. But alas, his tenure was short lived as he was reassigned to a different department that required his expertise. In fact, Dean was so impressed by Mr Kim that they still keep in touch until today, even holidaying together with their families.

Then Marcus took over from Mr Kim. He was one who would always have time to talk and always encouraged everyone to open up and let him know how he could help. He would take time to deliberate the matter and offer solutions. Never one to procrastinate, he would make decisions within a quick time frame. He was as decisive as he was reasonable. What was even better was that he would make time and frequently accompany the salespeople to see difficult customers to resolve problems head on. Soft spoken and mild tempered, he would lead all with his experiences and hands-on approach.

Unfortunately for Marcus, his past caught up with him. From the sketchy narrative that he volunteered, all were led to believe his gentle demeanour belied his coloured past. According to his own account, he would be clubbing through the night, and without having slept a wink, he would proceed to work as a teacher, his previous job. One wondered how he was able to stand up, let alone teach. In any case he survived as a teacher for some time.

His love for commerce saw him giving up his teaching career to take up positions with relatively big companies. Marcus was a brilliant thinker and an equally adept strategist. He was responsible for the start-up of some new divisions in some companies that are still very much alive today.

After some years as Dean's boss, his health deteriorated rather quickly to a point that he had to opt for softer work. He left the company and went into financial services. He did well and was rewarded with a company car. But it was a wrong move, as contrary to his expectation, the stress level in the financial services was worse. He resigned, and before long he fell ill and left the world to his final resting place.

Another boss, named Aaron, when Dean worked for Phoenix Inc., had a management style that ought to be applauded. Dean learnt a great deal about how to be professionally objective from Aaron. Dean's department was involved in the justification to purchase a new computer system. A committee was set up. Different sections were involved. Each would have his respective representative in the committee, and each would have his own set of ideas about the eventual outcome and how to make full use of the new system. With each section digging in their own agenda, flare-ups can be expected. If not properly managed, personal feelings could come into play. Dean had an assistant who strongly disagreed with the chairperson of the committee, the IT manager. Of course no one thought anything would come of this, until Dean was summoned to Aaron's office one morning. It was like a tribunal. Dean was alone, and Aaron had three others who were on his side.

"I will have none of this bickering in the office about the purchase of the new computer system. I will not have anyone sabotaging the recommendation!" Aaron did this slamming his fist on the table for emphasis.

Dean was shocked, as he never expected such harshness.

After Aaron said what he wanted to say, Dean then, with great composure, asked for permission to respond. And responded he did. He told him that no one was out to sabotage the purchase of the new computer system, most of all his department. For due diligence to be in place, Dean continued, differences of opinion must be allowed to surface in order not to miss out on any matter which could be important enough to be considered. Differences of opinions must also be given the latitude of an open discussion. They could only do this before the purchase to assess which vendor would be best to offer what would be the most suitable for the whole company. No one was out to subvert the process or the purchase. Dean was prepared to put his job on the line on this conviction.

When all had been considered, they would be fully aware of the possible outcome and consequences and to deal with them before it was too late. It was like scenario building.

After the purchase, Dean reassured Aaron that he could see no reason why anyone within the company, especially those who would stand to benefit greatly with the new installation, would want to do company in. All were end users too.

The after-effect of Dean's response was evident. After the meeting Aaron put his arm around him, and they talked shop for some time. Dean believed that was Aaron's way of apologizing for his unnecessary outburst.

On reflection, Dean felt that Aaron later rewarded him with a trip for a very important exhibition, and they had a whale of a time.

Under Aaron's able stewardship the company thrived. Team spiritedness was evident. He would organize sporting events including golf outings, and the company even had trophies for these annual events. There were exchange games across national borders. So much camaraderie formed the strongest foundation for the company.

Forgettable Junction—the "Greatest" Teachers of All Time, Hypocrisy and All

"How dare you learn to smoke?" That was followed by a big slap that remained indelibly etched in Dean's mind. That was a long time ago. In his teens, all his kampong friends were itching to sample the inhalation and the supposed high that came with the cigarette smoke descending into and killing the cells in their lungs. Dean's elder brother Danny, who had already graduated to self-confessed addicted smoker, caught him with his friends initiating into what was thought to be coming of age. He caught them red-handed, complete with cigarettes in their mouths and of course the accompanying bouts of a mixture of laughter and coughs. The slap was less painful than the social embarrassment in front of his close friends.

Little did he realize that was his first lesson of the famous adage "Do what I say, not what I do" that would endure through his journey in life. In fact, it can be witnessed no less by corporate bigwigs who would not flinch to embrace this philosophy. Some would even go so far as to even quote this line in their town hall meetings. Hypocrisy of the highest office shall be elaborated later.

It was during Dean's early teen years, after the smoking incident, that formed his later philosophy of life. The turning point was when his classmates prompted him to join the Church's Altar Boys Society. Days when he was not assigned to serve Mass, he would still frequently attend the service, some weeks even daily, and among the other things that he prayed hard for would be for him to obtain a Grade One in his GCE O-level examinations. God answered his prayers. He did okay and was accepted into Pre-U, or what is now called HSC or Junior College.

He never smoked since then, save a couple of times in America when in the heat of winter he was led to believe smoking during a beer-drinking session would make him feel warmer. How wrong that was!

The "greatest" teacher of all time for Dean was one by the name of Chia Kow Sai, whom he would always remember for as long as he lived. That was one to whom the crown as the "best" in imparting principles on "How not to be like him" rightly belonged to. He would be one typical person who would lose no time admonishing anyone who dared speak too much during a meeting. One suspected there was a certain air of insecurity behind the confident façade.

Kow Sai would even go so far as to say, "Who is chairing the meeting, you or me?" In other words, "Shut your gap! I am the only one to speak. I am chairing the meeting. You listen!" The strangest thing about that man was that he would at other times encourage everyone to speak up: "Otherwise we can never improve." An obvious contrarian or a typical hypocrite?

Annual increment was due. There were about ten managers who were huddled into a conference room, where Kow Sai would be chairing. He had a master list of all the staff under him including those, whom Dean guessed, he did not even know existed.

Kow Sai went on his rounds. "Mister so and so, how much are you recommending for this fellow?" All the colleagues would go on a selling spiel extolling the virtues and greatness of their immediate subordinates to support their recommendation. His response was a constant refrain: "Was this not expected of him?" up to a point all his colleagues would yield to his interrogative mode. One by one would just allow him to steamroll over their recommended salary increments for all their staff. This guy had a preconceived idea as to what each staff should get.

Dean's turn came up. Having had the prior advantage to see how he had treated everyone before him, he was adamant not to yield to him but to engage him even at his own peril. It did not matter as it was his staff he was fighting for. It was worth it. So he began his recommendations, and before he could finish, Kow Sai would, as usual, interject with the same, "Was this not expected of him?"

Dean let that irritation pass, but not for long when he decided that enough was enough and responded accordingly, "Kow Sai, if you continue with this argument, then why do you need us to sit down here to justify our recommendation, when you have obviously made up your mind who should get what? Further, please give me some credit for knowing my staff better than you, as I work with them everyday, whereas you don't."

You could hear a pin drop. Suddenly everybody was more interested in what was on the carpeted floor instead of looking at Kow Sai and Dean. Kow Sai gallantly responded, "Fair enough."

Dean felt victorious. Little did he realize he was in deep shit with this guy. He had been embarrassed in front of all the first-line managers, and beneath that veneer was a man with a vengeance. Surely he would begin his plot to make Dean suffer and eventually to eliminate him, regardless of how good a performer or hard worker he might be.

The lesson here was that while Dean won a small battle, it slowly dawned on him the effects of losing the war. He was foolhardy enough to stand up to his principles to challenge his manager. There was no question about the fact that Dean was right and Kow Sai was wrong, but he had chosen a public forum to show him up, and Kow Sai would not forget it, less so to let it pass without doing something about it.

Dean defaulted on the basic principle of respecting the individual and would then have to bite his tongue. He did not and would never respect him, which explained the spontaneity of his response. Although Kow Sai did not deserve the respect, Dean's failure was choosing the wrong platform to engage him, to his own detriment.

When you need to hire new staff for your immediate reports, would you not consider letting him do the interview for the first cut or at least let him know before deciding for him? Once, Dean came back from leave only to be told by Kow Sai that he had already engaged someone for him. The same happened to Dean at yet another company, and with which he responded with an immediate resignation, preferring to set up his own company where he would not have to contend with the likeness of such.

Dean's small cubicle was located beside Kow Sai's, so they shared a common partition. Often enough he would give the common partition violent punches or violent kicks when he wanted to see Dean for the most trivial of excuses. Had the punches or kicks been an iota more, one would be able to see Kow Sai's limbs protruding through the partition. That was how forceful the punches and kicks were. Colleagues who bore witness to this could only shake their heads with sympathy. No one had ever experienced such indignity and impoliteness in their entire lives. Dean admitted there were times he was tempted to make a quick run to the toilet as a weak excuse that he was not in his room and therefore did not hear the presumptuously rude knocks and kicks on the common partition. The diminishing bravado in Dean that came with age and heavier family commitment held him back, so the long journey of insults and demeaning began. Sleeplessness was his constant companion. It was then Dean knew the meaning of stress. But he was and still is blessed with an excellent listener and supporter in his wife, Bridget, who would accompany his de-stressing car rides in the middle of the night listening intently to the endless commentaries of his plight for hours on end with comforting words. That helped.

But that also taught him about something else. Bravery and boldness has an inverse relationship with increasing commitment. The bigger the family, the more humble pies you have to eat. In order to circumvent this problem, make solidly sure you have "quit money" stashed before engaging in any warfare, big or small.

Since he was young, Dean had held on to the belief that to be punctual for any meeting or even any social occasion is not only the right thing to do but shows how much respect you have for others. It is not fair for those who arrived early to be made to wait. The time wasted multiplied by the number of attendees could amount to some staggering figures, which, when converted into financial terms, can be quite a tidy sum. It is a good habit that he had translated into what he would loosely categorize as "leading by example."

Kow Sai was never on time, much less early, to work. But during the infrequent times he did arrive early enough and seeing that quite a few were late, he would break into a mood swing that all would rather forget. He would station himself at the doorway into the office and interrogate the latecomers. None could offer a good answer. It was later that all chanced upon the reason why he was early to work on that particular day. He had to bring his son to school, so he had to be early. Talk about one of the most basic of principles of management—walk the talk! Indeed!

During one of his meetings, Kow Sai informed all the managers that the company would like to relocate and mentioned a possible location that would have been nearer to Dean's home. Dean was happy to hear this, and his uncontrolled juvenile glee incensed Kow Sai so much that he berated Dean that he was so selfish and never had the interest of the company at heart. For example, he said, he never helped look for some other cheaper and better locations for the company. Who was Dean and at the level where he was? Would he be involved to even so much as offer suggestions?

Examples abound.

Poor Dean was on leave, and being a parent of school-going children, he had to plan the trips to coincide with school holidays. The planned trip to Malaysia was supposed to be a reprieve for the whole family, as he had chosen a slow drive up north. Upon arriving at his destination, he was given a message to call Kow Sai. When he came on the line he told Dean to return to the office and cancel the remaining part of his leave as he was required to do an urgent and important task.

Dean was quite elated that his service was required so urgently. He thought he must be quite important and indispensable. Of course he cut short his holiday and dutifully returned to the office, only to be told he would like Dean to take over the selling of one product, which deadline was way, way off.

On another occasion Dean applied for leave way in advance with all his family members in the know for a planned holiday together. Kow Sai would cancel the leave after approving it earlier, stating the company required him to do something, to sell yet another product which deadline was not even critical, and Dean and his family were going to be away for only seven days. He got the company to compensate him for the advance payment he had made. There was nothing about compensating the disappointment he had created for all the family members who had been looking forward to the holiday together.

There was one time when the company decided to undertake a special project as part of a service to the nation. The company needed to seek sponsors to help defray the cost of the project. Kow Sai made an announcement during one of the daily meetings that the project required connections, as it would be a relatively difficult sell because it was a pro-government initiative. Since he had a network of bigwigs of the corporate world with whom he frequently wined and dined, he declared that he was best positioned to do the deed. So it was, or so all thought. Weeks passed and no one was aware of the progress that he had made—or the lack thereof.

Then one day out of the blue, Dean was summoned to his office and it was there that he asked Dean to take over the project. No problem. Dean said he would gladly do it. "When is the deadline?" he asked.

"Two days' time," came the shocker.

How to do the impossible, yet Dean told him he would do his best. The following day Dean came back with a contract, much to Kow Sai's amazement. Talk about talking big!

Entertaining clients in the evening was quite common. There were days that Dean would be required to be present. On one evening, Kow Sai had Dean with him and they were entertaining some Korean clients. It was after dinner, and they adjourned for some drinks, as was the usual routine. Dean was a tad better than a teetotaller, which was public knowledge. If you cut Kow Sai's veins, you would not find blood but alcohol.

Dean was given a shot of whiskey, which he would be able to handle if he was given the latitude to nurse throughout the evening.

But Kow Sai would have none of that. "Come on, bottoms up," he said, directing Dean, who pretended not to hear or understand him and so he took a sip, much to Kow Sai's wrath.

Dean's sheepish plea that he could not drink fell on deaf ears, although Kow Sai was fully aware of his inability to oblige. He retorted, "Why do you not want to give me face in front of our client?" loud enough for the Korean client to get a full load of, and at the same time preferring to subject Dean to the likelihood of not being able to drive home safely in one piece.

Broken and dispirited, Dean had no choice but to down the entire contents. He was *high* but managed to reach home. But he could not even untie his shoes upon reaching home. Bridget had to help. He slumped into the sofa in the hall to catch a breather for some time before retiring to bed without a shower. Bridget and Dean would never forget this episode, nor forgive Kow Sai. He had no respect for anybody. He knew only to enjoy himself. It did not matter if his staff had to suffer.

Kow Sai invited quite a few clients, who through business became friends, to dinner, and as usual they adjourned for some drinks after dinner. That time it was at some sleazy outfit where misbehaviour was encouraged. Such places would understandably levy a heavy premium for the extra-special and out-of-the-ordinary services. The bill for that night out was therefore not low. So how do you claim for reimbursement from the company when the receipt would have been an easy giveaway and would result in a credibility issue born out of indiscretion for Kow Sai. Better not risk that. So he decided not to pay and directed his subordinate to settle first and then to take his family out for as many dinners as required up to the amount as a payback and to submit such claims to him for his approval.

Now how would one reconcile with that?

Dean commenced making a journal of all those unhappy incidents, and armed with them he confronted Kow Sai twice. Of course Kow Sai was in denial, attributing Dean's feeling to his being sensitive. Was he? His unrelenting harshness knew no bounds. His words and actions were no different. He would quote the phrases and words that Dean used in his reports for public humiliation during meetings.

Once Kow Sai called Dean to his office and told him he had received a complaint that one of the staff under him misbehaved in front of the client and told him to reprimand him. Of course he would do his bidding in this instance. The company's image should never be compromised. Dean summoned this guy and gave him a telling off that drove him to tears. He complained to Kow Sai, who in turn called and chided Dean for overreacting.

Confronted with these streaks of unreasonableness, Dean gathered enough courage to see Howard, Kow Sai's boss, at the risk of a possible peril. He began by stating the facts that he loved working for the company and that the company had been very good to him, but he could no longer work with Kow Sai anymore. It was sincere and never meant to disparage. The company sponsored Dean to further his education and frequently sent him to numerous seminars and courses overseas. Dean wondered whether Kow Sai ever had a hand in this. Doubtful! Dean then detailed in his journal the many times he'd had to suffer in silence.

The company was and is very good, but unfortunately, it was people with such low EQs that made lives so miserable for so many. The irony was that such managers were allowed to survive and fly below the company radar and would even be rewarded, all in the name of slave driving for the company's interest.

Howard then asked how it could be possible for Kow Sai to treat Dean so badly when he actually recommended him to take over a foreign office. (The method he'd adopted regarding this was to station Dean in a foreign country, full time and alone, with only a monthly trip home. Dean rightly asked that if not his whole family at least his wife should be allowed to accompany him there since it was a full-time assignment. The reply was a firm *no*. Dean then recommended another colleague, but he turned down the offer as well.)

Soon after, another colleague, much junior in service, was given the position. His whole family, with three or four adult children, went along. It was suspected that the schooling of the children was taken care of by the company, but what was quite definite was that all the children were educated there. How could it be possible for any wage earner to be able to afford to send three or four adult children to foreign schools and universities if not for generous subsidies from companies? That guy had a swell time for a good number of years when the original offer to Dean was very different.

Why the difference?

Once Kow Sai was unhappy about the competition, he began challenging Dean's colleague, Bernard, as to why he was unable to convert a particular client. Bernard offered an explanation, and to lend weight to his point, Dean supported Bernard—and the focus swiftly was no longer on Bernard, who got away, but on poor Dean, who had the raw end of the stick for sticking out his head for an issue that was not his to talk about. Kow Sai turned on Dean and made sure Dean regretted opening his mouth.

Kow Sai's management style was highly unusual. He was an avid golfer and would sing praises about how deals could be struck on the course. In order to get everyone interested, he organized golfing clinics and got quite a few interested in the game. He declared to all that playing golf with clients during office hours would be considered working and therefore application for leave was not required. But when some of the staff had graduated with the proper handicap to host some golf games during weekdays, he would ask that they apply for leave.

After a while he decided Dean should buy a golf club membership. He did so without even consulting him and did not care whether Dean was financially able to afford one. He came to his cubicle, used his phone, negotiated with the seller, and finally agreed on the buying price, totally oblivious that Dean was right in front of him, only separated by a distance equivalent to the width of the desk. Dean told him categorically that he would not be able to pay for the membership, so he made arrangements with the company to pick up the tab first, and then Dean had to suffer six months of instalments for something he had no say in buying.

Not long after Dean's secret meeting with Kow Sai's boss, Howard, another colleague, Andrew Loh, and Dean were called to Kow Sai's room. He got up to close his door and pushed a sealed letter to each of them with the order, "Open it!" So they did. It was then that both realized they were promoted. It was the most unglamorous promotion exercise anyone could ever have.

On such occasions, one could expect some kind of pep talk preceding the handing of the promotion letter. But that was not Kow Sai's style. In any case, would anyone want to be promoted to work directly under him? After all the scars Dean was inflicted with over the years, he searched for answers and could not even sleep a wink that night. He wondered how many would share the same sentiments he did. Instead of rejoicing and celebrating, he was filled with anxiety.

The following day he asked to see Kow Sai and courageously handed the promotion letter back to him with the remark, "There could only be two possible reasons why a person is promoted. One is in recognition of his performance, and the other is to promote him up and out. You know we never worked well together and I believe I belong to the latter."

Kow Sai was furious. "You think this is fun and games? If I had wanted you out, it would have been quite easy for me to do that. You'd better take it back before I lose my temper."

Dean made his point and sentiments very clear and was glad he had the guts to do so. He sheepishly retreated and took the letter back, thereby sealing his own fate, working even more closely with the tyrant.

It was evident to all that Bernard was Kow Sai's heir apparent. In Kow Sai's absence he would appoint him to look after most of the duties, including the approving of leave and expense claims. It was so apparent that Dean sought out Bernard to congratulate him, remarking that soon Bernard would be his boss. They shook hands on that. Dean wanted to reassure Bernard of his sincerity and support, as they were peers. It was understandable that both parties would feel rather awkward. Today they are on par, and next day, one would be the subordinate of the other. But such is the reality of the corporate world. This can happen to anyone.

But the unthinkable happened. Dean was promoted instead of Bernard, who then had to report to him. This time Dean was the one who felt uncomfortable. He knew how Bernard must have felt. He later confided in Dean that he asked to speak to Kow Sai, who in turn abruptly declined granting him the meeting, saying to the effect that he preferred to deal with whatever issues on the phone as he was busy. It was obvious what the meeting was all about. He was bypassed, and any human would have felt slighted without a proper explanation.

The lesson here is, by all means make unpleasant decisions, and then run and hide as quickly as possible so you do not need to explain your actions to anyone. Easier that way. Judgment by silent jury is a much easier option!

Somehow Dean got this feeling that his secret meeting with Howard had something to do with the promotion exercise. The lesson here is never yield to bullying bosses, but bear in mind that you need evidence to support your case. Gather as much as possible, even the petty incidents, to strengthen your case. At the right time show your hand. It is worth the gamble. But be mentally prepared for any outcome. And of course financial independence would make a world of difference.

In any case Dean thought he'd had enough, and as he was headhunted to head a small company with a higher salary, he decided he should have a crack at it. So he quit. He had to give the usual three months' notice. About two weeks prior to his departure, the chairman of the company he was supposed to join had a discussion with him, and it was then that he realized it would have been a mistake if he had gone ahead to join that small company. The chairman, who was a friend and soon to be his boss, was no longer the same person Dean used to know. At one time he was gentle, kind, and seemingly very understanding. But as the time drew near for Dean to take up his position with the company, the chairman's attitude changed. Among other things, he was insistent that Dean submit his business plan way in advance of joining. Dean thought there was an apparent conflict of interest. The chairman's response was heavily tinged with sarcasm. Was that symptomatic of what was to come? No way was Dean going to jump from the frying pan into the fire. It would still be better to deal with a known devil than to jump into an unknown hell.

It was then that Dean asked Kow Sai about a possible U-turn. Kow Sai was gallant enough to accept the withdrawal of the resignation and reinstate Dean with no change of title. He assigned him new responsibilities. That was one redeeming act Kow Sai did for Dean, to which Dean was grateful.

As luck would have it, another senior colleague of a subsidiary company left and recommended that Dean take over his position. It was then that Dean steered away from Kow Sai's grasp. He no longer had to report to Kow Sai.

Since Dean was no longer under Kow Sai's management, he would be invited to have drinks with him on many occasions at his favourite haunt, which Dean suspected was his way to build an internal network to gather whatever input he may need time and again. It was during one of those sessions that Dean enquired the possibility of returning to his division. It was a tough decision that he had to make. He was not enjoying himself at the new place and was really torn between the devil and the deep blue sea.

His new boss typified what a boss should never be. How would one be able to perform under a management environment when the boss was more interested in keeping his bosses happy at the expense of his subordinates? This particular category of managers suffers from what is termed as "Testicular Syndrome," or TS. On the one hand, they lose no time fawning over their CEOs/chairman—to the extent of chauffeuring them and pandering to their whims and fancies, taking notes of their likes and dislikes, remembering their birthdays and the birthdays of their spouses, timely deliveries of gifts for such occasions, taking them to taste their favourite food at newly discovered F&B outlets, and the list goes on. Then on the other hand they avoid making nasty decisions when confronted with difficult or controversial issues. They are also infamous for breaking promises.

Internal conflicts were swept under the carpet, hoping that with the passage of time the problem would just vanish into thin air. Well, that never happened, and some could even pose serious problems in the future if not nipped in the bud. And so it was a fateful decision for Dean to bail from the frying pan and into fire . . . because of TS.

Unfortunately, TS is a common disease among bullies, masquerading as effective managers hiding behind macho appearances. Look around any corporation and you will be able to smoke them out quite easily. Those whose demeanour changes rapidly from that of a lion in front of their subordinates to that of a mouse with the sudden appearance of their bosses would typify sufferers of this syndrome. When it came to the crunch, one can witness the wilting of a man. Never rely on such creatures to bail you out. These would be the ones to approve your budgets or plans. They can even go to the extent of praising your well-thought-out plans but not when the board rejects them. Support from these pseudo-managers would vanish at the most crucial moments. They ignore you even when you attempt to seek moral support by establishing eye contact in the boardroom. You stand alone. You fend for yourself. They don't know you.

And what was worse was that some would not hide their wanton penchant for "skirts." Good-looking "skirts" would be given special treatment, never mind the bonuses. Even decisions with a more serious commercial implications were made with the latter factor playing a dominant part. Confronted with this dilemma, Dean had to decide. What was uppermost in his mind was to have a greater peace of mind, so he made a comeback to Kow Sai . . . pity! A lesson in itself.

Kow Sai accepted Dean's application to return, much to his surprise. Obviously Dean was mad to ask to return to the lion's den to be mauled yet again. How much more masochistic would one want to be? The week before he went back to work for Kow Sai's division he had a meeting with him, and it was then that Dean asked where his work station would be. Preferring to adopt an even more serious look in his response to Dean, Kow Sai pointed to the sofa in his room as Dean's work station. That was humiliating! It could only mean that there was no place for Dean whatsoever. It was insulting! It was then that Dean knew he had it yet again. He'd asked for it. No more!

Call it youthful ignorance or what you may, but Dean never wanted to work with Kow Sai ever again, and so ended one memorable junction of his working life.

In another encounter in his journey through life, Dean had the misfortune of working with yet another tyrant. Dean was called by this manager, Chia Ngeow Sai, for a meeting in his office. With a name like that, Dean suspected he must be a relative of Chia Kow Sai, but he never researched their roots to support his theory. Ngeow Sai had just been installed for barely three months. Approaching the office, Dean was greeted by the waft of fresh glue. He remembered that he felt a little high. New carpets were just laid.

"New carpet?" Dean enquired.

"Do you like it?" Ngeow Sai asked.

"Frankly, I don't." *Shit! What did I just say?* Dean thought.

Ngeow Sai asked, "Why?"

Dean's rejoinder dug himself into a deeper hole. The carpet had this wavy design that gave him a nauseated feeling somewhat similar to sea sickness, and he was foolish enough to tell him so. And as if to further compound the gravity of his impetuousness, Dean asked how Ngeow Sai was going to reconcile with the shop floor when they just had a salary reduction exercise in the name of cost savings. To top it all, the carpet had not needed changing. It was still usable.

His reply was that Dean did not understand the importance of image and that his office was the corporate office and was therefore the face of the company, where guests, especially overseas guests, would get a first impression. So management by example had to take a backseat. If he was unhappy with Dean, he hid his feelings well, but Dean knew he was doomed to hell.

Imagine within a span of 30 minutes meeting, Dean dug himself into an irrecoverable abyss. To put in mildly, he was a goner.

Did he learn anything from that episode? Of course! One can be honest and true to oneself, but never fall prey to impetuousness. In such instances, hypocrisy will pay high dividends. With the wisdom of hindsight, Dean should have affirmed Ngeow Sai's decision that the carpet needed replacing as it was worn out and that he had good taste. Then he should have bitten his tongue and swallowed the blood in honour of hypocrisy and his survival. His bruised tongue would have saved the day. Then he could seek treatment through the company's medical programme to look after his sore tongue. Fortune would have been drastically altered with spilt blood.

Hypocrisy among bigwigs was and still is very fashionable. "My, what a beautiful dress you have!" can be heard among socialites, at cocktail circuits, when in reality the design of the dress was dated, the colour was off, the material was cheap looking. What is even more fashionable is that such remarks should be accompanied with the glow of a toothy Colgate smile while at the same time maintaining a straight face of hypocritical sincerity.

In town hall meetings, when confronted with searching queries, choose to be politically correct even if you had just endorsed an executive order to retrench. Yet when asked, "Will there be a retrenchment soon?" just say no, and reassure everyone that job security is of paramount importance and "we will look at ways to redeploy people, put them where their expertise will matter, retraining those who need it, and we will try our very best to retain as many as possible." Here of course the caveat is the bit on "retaining as many as possible," which would best be delivered with the lowest decibel of a whisper, but making sure that important phrase was recorded.

Management by example is one dictum that is best demolished by wantonness. You have no prior experience in this line of work yet by some big stretch of imagination you were appointed, so why not ask for the sky? High take-home salary be a given. How about asking for something more visible? Something that will let the world know you have arrived, not demised, especially when you have just been sidelined? How about a big car? Never mind that I so happen to own one of the same stature, which can be left at home—after all, I have enough car park spaces at home to cater for two of the same make. I need this as it will enhance my mobility to move from one location of the company's complex to the next, which may be as far away as five hundred metres! Even though all my predecessors had to make do with more modest hand-me-downs, it is okay even as the company is bleeding, even if retrenchment and pay cuts would need to be implemented, otherwise how will the company afford these perks for me? After all, I did not apply for the job, I was appointed.

"Don't worry; I will protect you, but you must do the needful—otherwise I will not be able to continue to defend you!" Platitudes! "Do the needful"? What is "doing the needful"? It is as good as saying that if you do not do your job well, never mind, the market is in the doldrums, prepare your own exit.

Respect for an individual is best abused by walking into the office of your immediate subordinate and asking the subordinate's juniors questions like, "Tell me what's going on here. Is there anything I should know?" This was done in full view of the subordinate's office. What better way to subvert the confidence of your people than to let all know there is a divide-and-conquer attitude that is encouraged and politicized. Frankly, one cannot think of anything more damaging to the immediate subordinates' confidence than this.

Budget-setting time is by far the most dreaded moment of corporate life. You can spend days on end coming up with rationales and figures. Justification—some real, some pure imagination—would have been deployed. Sometimes the company could very well be in a monopolistic position, yet when a new player is in town, it should not matter, and that was what some companies would like to adopt as a philosophy, one that is oblivious to market conditions. When there are more players in the market providing the same service, it is reasonable to expect a shrinking of the market share, all things being equal (more so in a small market). With the boldness of not factoring in the effect of an additional player in the setting of the sales target and brave enough to forecast a small increase of, say 5 per cent over the previous year, when there was no competition, was not approved is one frustrating exercise.

Came the directive, "We need 23 per cent increase over the previous year!" Common sense will tell you that if the new competitor were to erode as little as 30 per cent market share from the incumbent, a mere 5 per cent increase is really working the market up by some 35 per cent. Asking for a 23 per cent increase would mean the market size must go up by 53 per cent. Now that is what is called totally beyond challenging and an exercise in futility.

To satisfy the curiosity with regard to how the company would have done at the close of the financial year, it was revealed that the revenue actually went down by 23 per cent. Now that was reality. Well, that was one ambitious directive, which was doomed to death from the very start.

Talking about an idiot leading the company—one that was totally inexperienced and would tell the world that the top position in any company only needed common sense to manage and to leave the technical know-how to the subordinates. That was one fine example of how to waste company funds by the subscription of the famous expression "blind leading the blind." The best way to do this is to appoint an ignoramus that would turn to the most obvious way out by reaching for a foreign talent (which was fashionable) that would ostensibly be able to provide the expertise. Now if this foreigner was worth his salt, then why the need for him to engage yet another foreigner as yet another crutch to manage the company? It does not require a rocket scientist to see that these three blind men would set the company back by millions. This is excellent fodder for a possible case study for Harvard MBA programmes.

Will companies ever learn that if there are reasons imposed by the board why such high targets are necessary, to involve all the departmental heads and explain the need for such a high target? Never mind even if that was a top-down approach. Be it because there was a sudden increase in the expatriate headcount (foreign talents) with benefits thrown in, like staying in service apartments, engaging freelancers at high costs because foreign talents were needed as crutches, and that there was this new learning curve that so many of the new heads were going through, would have gone a long way to gain some support to go for the high targets and higher bottom line, never mind the cynicism. These could well have gotten some sympathetic support, albeit a small one. That would still be better than none and honesty would have been applauded. And even if the top line was impossible, the bottom line could still be a possibility. That could be achieved through concerted efforts and everybody buying in, to cut costs.

If the company had in mind a figure to achieve, why waste so much resources and man hours only to hand out an impossible edict later, disregarding all the ancillary work that had to be done only to declare them useless by default? Even more important, sleepless nights could have been avoided. And with creativity and imagination, these nights could have been converted to more productive use.

All of us are fully aware that there will always be what is termed a "buffer game" in all budget preparation, all for the common good. The board may ask for a 10 per cent increase, but management will insist on a 15 per cent increase from all the operational levels, who in turn would call for nothing less than 20 per cent improvement from all the sectional heads. At the end of the day the poor slaves will get the raw end to deliver the higher number in order to achieve their commission.

And at the end of the year with the actual results in and there was the 10 per cent increase which was the original target in the first place. Here is the underlying weakness of the "buffer game" as the poor slaves would have been deprived of their commission, but the management and board would be congratulating each other for their fine performance, with the chief's bonus being further enhanced. How unfair and unreasonable can you be?

The difference that sets true-blue companies apart from the rest is that they listen to feedback from the ground up. These can be reaffirmed by giving the operational level some latitude to come up with realistic figures. Tweaking the numbers is acceptable, but when the difference is as wide as 23 to 53 per cent, something is not quite right. Do not force-feed just to glory seek. It will boomerang, to much regret.

Another boss Dean had the opportunity to work with was one brilliant guy named Martin. He epitomized the high IQ and low EQ. Under him the company went through what could be loosely defined as a metamorphosis of sorts. He worked passionately and tirelessly for the company, which had historic growth under him. He orchestrated so many new ventures that saw the company's profile progressively improving, even in the region. Unfortunately, he fell prey to the politics he had unwittingly engendered. A poor judge of character, he had groomed a "Brutus" to his own regret, as he openly admitted.

It would not be wrong to say selflessness and energy levels are two very clear leadership traits for senior managers. Martin would conduct meetings after meetings and would leave the office in the wee hours of the morning only to find himself one of the first to be in the office of the same morning. He would sacrifice his meals to make sure things were in order. He never seemed to care much about taking advantage of the company. He never asked for a bigger car and was happy to accept a hand-me-down regardless of the age or the make. He was only interested in improving the top line, bottom line, and the status of the company. Truly a gem of a corporate man.

But he had two major problems: his ears and his very poor judgement of character. His ears were so light that any attempt to hang earrings would result in severing his human antenna. He allowed himself to be manipulated, preferring to listen to only one Brutus who would be rewarded for whatever he was doing. In fact, the two would have been seen together in and out of the office day and even in the evening. He had a de facto number two.

However, selflessness was his forte. He would stop at nothing to do good for the company. But his sense of insecurity got the better of him, and he would be worried about loyalty and would be quite explicit in asking for it. If he were so much as to detect a hint of a possible drift of allegiance, he would not waste time in handing out treatment of equal measure and pain.

In meetings he would frequently be found venting his frustration about anything that displeased him, using very strong words like, "Sack that guy!" And so it was thought that dismissing staff would seem a very casual task for him. But he barked more than he bit, as he never fired anyone. Martin preferred to drive those whose loyalty was in question to the brink until they voluntarily yielded and resigned on their own. But there were those whose resilience or just plain luck that their fortune could turn for them, in which case he would just accept the status quo. On the other hand, if anyone were to be gutsy enough to confront or challenge him, he would back down. In the company all seemed to concur on this trait.

One time Dean submitted an expense claim for his travels, which, according to the HR department, kept reappearing in the out tray without his signature. It would be reasonable to assume that the manager had chosen not to approve the claim. That apparently happened quite a few times, until the HR manager told Dean to deal with him directly, which he did.

In his analysis, Dean thought the manager was unhappy over his travel plans for whatever reasons and asked to see him. "I understand my expense claim kept coming out into your out tray without your approval. Is there a problem?" Dean did that with the seriousness of a fighter.

He responded with a very innocent and childlike look. "No! I must have missed it," and just as quickly approved the reimbursement.

Known for his enterprising spirit, he tried his hand to do his own business with some promise, with as big a fanfare for the opening as was its closure.

Integrity

Since having left the corporate world and starting his own little outfit, Dean had learnt to embrace *integrity* as one of the important hallmarks in whatever he did. Say what you mean and mean what you say. Never lie! During company briefings, when a relevant issue cropped up, his anecdotes illustrated his points on integrity, cautioning his staff of the pitfalls of not being honest.

If you lie, you have to remember a few things. You must consistently remember the lie and pray you will not be found out later. You may have to tell more lies to cover the first one, which means you need a huge CPU to track this, otherwise cracks will appear and you may find yourself in some hot soup. Backpedaling is one humongous task when you invariably put your dignity, credibility, and self-respect on the line. If you tell the same lie often enough, very soon you will buy the lie and will believe it's now the "truth." Do we really want that to happen to us, trifling with our integrity, which has a bearing on our future?

Integrity can never be earned but can only be lost. It is not wrong to say integrity is always taken for granted. Nobody expects anyone to steal, as it is presumed one should not take what does not belong to him. Therefore, by turning away and not stealing, we have not earned integrity. It is expected. But by succumbing to temptation, we have lost our honour and, therefore, our integrity. This is irreversible. It is not possible to wind back the clock to undo what you had done, nor can you gouge out this piece of dirt from the minds of those who came to know about it. An indelible dirt much to be regretted!

So in his small outfit and in the previous companies of the corporate world. he tried to impart this to all who worked with him. His constant rejoinder was always, are you defensible? In his business practice upon their request, clients' invoices would be attached with third-party invoices so they would know nothing was amiss. If for some reason or another a credit note was issued by his supplier, his client would be similarly credited. Such practices are rare in the industry. But his reasoning was that it would set his company apart from all the others. So far he had managed to more than survive. He had been told this philosophy would never make him rich—money-wise, that is—but that would make the company and him rich in many other ways, reputation for one.

Another example is Hong who obviously manifested a total lack of integrity, once worked for a database company, one of those that sold names and addresses to credit cards, luxury brands, banks, etc. for a fee. In other words, Hong would have access to the list and the complete profile of quite a few people. Very proudly he declared he was able to data mine the list to seek out well-heeled divorcees and widows. In fact, he dated quite a few of them. He was very proud of this achievement.

Hong was married for twenty-five years and had two children, and it was apparent that he had wilfully chosen not to leave his philandering ways behind. He switched jobs quite often, and in one company he had to contend with the embarrassment of a poison letter about his alleged affairs, which was circulated to all and sundry within the company. He was immediately dismissed.

All of us are human and are prone to make mistakes. Even the most intelligent and highest-paid CEO would not be spared. As bosses, we must be tolerant to mistakes our staff make. The proviso depends on the seriousness of the mistakes and the nature as well. Fair dealing would require us to undertake some due diligence processes prior to forming a conclusion. If the mistake should set the company back with huge losses, then the conclusion is obvious. If it was not that serious, then counselling could be conducted to ensure no repeat. Despite that, a repeat may be committed, and it can be concluded that no lesson was ever learnt by that person.

Dean liked to use the analogy of how one could burn a finger to satisfy one's curiosity to know what the flickering flame of a candle was like and still choose to burn yet another finger over a stove as not having learnt anything. Worst still was the unwillingness to learn. Forgiveness should never be meted out in this instance.

Once Bob was very unhappy with his employer and confided his feelings with Din Teo, who was then running his own design company with a staff of about fifteen. Din was doing fairly well, and upon hearing his plight, he made Bob an impetuous offer to work for him. Bob was overjoyed to say the least and started making plans to leave the current company to join Din. In fact, he was at the brink of submitting his resignation but held back just in case. His prudence paid off.

After the offer, Bob made a dinner appointment with Din, hoping to finalise the offer and discuss his start date. Dinner was at 7.00 p.m. At about 6.00 Bob made a call to Din, who did not take the call, and had to reconfirm the dinner appointment with Din's secretary. It was confirmed. The secretary confirmed that Din was aware and that he was also given a reminder.

It was not until 8.00 p.m. that Bob realized he had been stood up by Din. The following morning Bob called Din, who claimed ignorance and whose excuse was that it was the wrong day. Din's secretary disagreed. So the dinner was postponed to another day, during which time Bob candidly told Din that if the job offer was inconvenient it would be okay, as he had yet to resign from his current position. Din insisted it was okay, so Bob submitted all the documents, including his salary slips to substantiate his salary base. With all those duly done, Bob never heard from Din again.

It was this episode that Bob recalled when Din approached Bob to help him headhunt a suitable candidate to fill a vacancy that a similar situation arose. Repeated phone calls from the interviewee after the interview went unanswered. Promises by Din's secretaries that Din would call back never happened. Candidates were suspended in limbo, not knowing the outcome of their interview. Even those genuinely seeking answers were met with deafening silence.

The question is why do some so-called CEOs behave this way?

Many suggested that not all CEOs are confident enough to confront unpleasantness. So the easy way out is to avoid the issue and pray that time will resolve what they humanly cannot handle.

Hallmarks of a Leader

There are obvious hallmarks of a leader like;
1. Be selfless,
2. Has high energy level,

3. Keeps his word,
4. Savvy,
5. Has integrity,
6. Is well informed,
7. Is well connected,
8. Is willing to help,
9. Is willing and daring to confront tough and unpleasant situations and
10. Is prepared make tough and unpopular decisions.

Let us look at some of these and understand why the above characteristics are important, with good and bad examples, although in the preceding chapters some of these have been amply described.

Integrity figures very highly in this scheme of things and has been duly touched on in the preceding chapter.

Dean was once appointed CEO of a small loss-making company (a subsidiary of a bigger organization) with the objective of turning it around. In his first briefing with the staff, he issued a warning that all was not well and urged all to help pull the company from the red. He gave them six months to get their act together, failing which salary reduction will be emplaced in order to keep the company afloat. After six months, the company was still in the red. That was when he acted upon his warning—to cut salaries. The salary reduction formula that he adopted was to stagger the reduction in percentage. His salary being the highest had the highest reduction 10%, and then the rest staggered in 5% intervals. The lowest salaried staff was given an exemption. He kept his word and carried out what he promised that he would do. Not long after this exercise, the company started turning around.

There is no question that whoever seeks to be popular will never make a good and effective CEO. There will always be issues that need decisive actions for the greater good of the company that he runs. Invariably there will be some that will be popular and some unpopular. The latter takes a toll on the emotions, and the weak of heart would prefer inaction and hope things would turn out well. In other words, leaving the matter to fate. Now the latter type typifies a weak manager who should never be a CEO.

Can you imagine a laggard on the team pulling down the performance and the morale of the organization— and the CEO is reluctant to remove him? Surely the opportunists would pounce on this and make sure this precedent would be duly cited when the time calls for it. How would an organization move from here? Except perhaps to go downhill.

The critical question is, how does one detect such characteristics in people? Apart from the personality profile testing, one observation is people's willingness to accept substandard services of anything, preferring to console themselves that patience is a virtue. Do not be mistaken!

As in the preceding chapter this Hong who held a middle-management position with few people working under him had a weird management style. It was clearly to leave all his staff alone. Upon being asked the reason for that approach, he was quick to say that one should never teach one's subordinates all the tricks of the trade lest they become better and may even take over your job. One wonders about his selflessness.

Wealth Management Junction

One important lesson is on how to manage one's sudden wealth. It could be a sudden windfall, a lottery win, or a huge legacy from parents. Like it or not, however educated one can be, the sudden euphoria can serve to blur a person's perspective of life. Here are two examples.

Mr Gan was married with two beautiful children and had been working for his family's business in charge of marketing for a good number of years. Business was good, and the company grew with many outlets, and branched out into many other businesses and was an obvious target for a takeover. A Malaysian tycoon had his eye on the company, and before long this company was assimilated into the Malaysian Group and was listed with the local stock exchange. Mr Gan became a millionaire overnight. Mr Gan was not too savvy with regard to investment, so he asked for help seeking investment opportunities. Since Dean had some banking contacts, he made some calls. Gan received some good advice and was on his way to even greater wealth.

After many years, Dean learnt he had quite a few properties around the region, which meant his worth had indeed multiplied. Good for him.

Conversely, Mr Foo had the great fortune of being bestowed millions from his father, who passed on. Dean happened to chance upon him when Foo was in his late thirties or early forties. Such casual encounters would usually descend to, "How are you doing and what are you doing now?"

Dean was taken aback when he was told by Foo that had chosen to retire, and the reason was that he was sick and tired of corporate politics and that he was then in a position of not having to work. For the former reasoning it was understandable, but for the latter Dean was not in agreement, as he has always believed nobody should ever retire however well off one is. For as long as one is healthy and not physically or medically disabled, one should continue to be economically active and to continue to contribute and to work the grey matter.

While some will agree with Dean preferring only to embark on social work instead, his contention was that social work is not the same. It does not engage as much of one's senses. Dean may be wrong here, but he happens to think the stress level from social work is not comparable to a commercial enterprise. When you win or lose an order, your adrenalin rush takes a different dimension. You will be compelled to strategize and look for ways to solve or salvage the situation when it calls for it. It is the challenge that gives you the high, which social work may not be able to offer. Corporate work works the brain harder than social work; it teases and tickles, whereas social work only pleases.

In any case, Dean lost touch with Foo for a while, and when he next enquired about him, he was told his wife divorced him and that he had chosen to work as a chauffeur just to make ends meet for him and his mother, who had chosen to live with him in a small apartment. He had squandered his millions. So sad!

Dean gathered that the first decision he'd made upon receipt of his millions was to buy a big limousine. Here it is important to delve a little deeper into this with an analysis. Why do you buy a limousine when any car will do? It must be a showpiece. After all, it says "I can afford one now," making true the psychographic description of "possession paraders" for this category of people. It follows therefore that in order to realize the "parade," the car must not be garaged but on the road for other road users to see, admire, gawk at, or envy. But you cannot just be seen driving it on the road alone and aimlessly. There must be the fawning oohs and aahs from friends to complete the ecstasy. What must not be forgotten is that you can't just invite friends for joy rides for the head-turning parade along Orchard Road; there must be a destination. Pubs of course. After all, "I am also into drinking now and then." A shot once or twice a week will not hurt. And so the two elements of inviting friends and the destination would automatically imply that you are the willing host for the nights out. So when the drinking bouts are over, guess who will reach for the bill? Not the apple-polishing freeloaders but the host, of course! Therein lies the viciousness of digging oneself into a rut of no return.

You like drinking and must have company, and the nicer the company the better, and as big spenders there is that special aura that tends to attract the gentler and dangerous kind. With free drinks, streams of gifts, and being seen in such an enviable limousine, who would not want such a debonair man for company? Slowly but surely a relationship will develop. It's a trap! Your marriage is in jeopardy. It will not be wrong to hazard a guess that some shopkeepers may even have a different price tags for such paraders. So parade, by all means, to your own peril.

The Discerning Junction

There was this guy, Richie, who was schooled into believing that one must be supportive of staff, groom them, help them all the way, train them if need be, and so on. Such is the only way to work yourself out of a job so that you can be promoted. Since his corporate stint of some thirty years, Richie was still looking for that bloke that instilled such a ludicrous idea in his head. Watch it! Now, the wisdom behind that thinking was that the ones you ought to look out for and don't give a damn about are those that appear meek and somewhat servile, very industrious, and who will swear their allegiance to you at a drop of a hat. They are the ones who will remember your birthdays, your wedding anniversary, and even your wife's birthday. Generous with gifts too. How else to gain some vantage points over the other colleagues for their own purpose?

Butch and Virginia were good friends, and together they felt tired of selling and wanted to branch into marketing. They even said that failing to get into marketing in the same company, the two would resign to seek greener pastures. Richie felt that instead of losing them to the outside world, he preferred to "lose" them in his department while retaining them by granting them the transfer for the greater benefit (and so he thought) of the company. He worked tirelessly with his boss to achieve the transfer. It was eventually done. So Richie thought he had two grateful friends for life.

All was fine and dandy for a couple of years—the brewing years, the initiating and weaning years for Butch and Virginia to win some brownie points for themselves.

Then their true colours began to show.

Richie was then heading sales when Butch and Virginia were in marketing. A product that had yet to be imported and which was still in negotiation was then touted as a done deal and was publicly announced as such. Richie received this rude shock when he was pressured to deliver a sales projection within a certain time frame, even though the contract to import the new product was not even concluded. When confronted, Butch and Virginia claimed ignorance. So began a rough road of divergent interest between two former team mates.

The inseparable duo had the benefit of a new boss who had no background of the business and was thus being led by the nose. A great opportunity to strengthen their position presented itself. Gifts flowed. Dinners with suppliers were frenziedly organized. Gullible bosses could be easily bought, and soon the two got what they had been gunning for, a promotion. Old friends no longer existed. They no longer mattered.

Richie happened to be invited to the same function as Butch and Virginia. All three were seated at the same table. Not a single word was exchanged; not even a simple hello was ever uttered. There was no effort to make eye contact throughout the one-hour dinner.

My friend wished them luck and fortune on their lives' journey . . .

Yet another example is Robert, a colleague of Thomas's. Both were senior staff of a big organization, heading different departments. Both would have regular drinks and meals and had through time developed a mutual support for each other.

One day Thomas decided to strike out on his own and needed a favour from Robert, whose brash response was, "Sorry, I'm afraid I cannot be of help." That clearly illustrated to all that "for as long as you are of use, I will be there, but when your usefulness has expired, I am afraid I cannot extend the same." Rightly too, as things were quite different after all. Thomas could no longer assist or at least be of help to Robert's aspiration within the organization.

We would invariably remember some characters in our lives whose company we do not really cherish, in particular those legendary "convenient toilet escapees," or the "excuse manufacturers" or the "ghost host."

Let me illustrate. There was a guy who would frequently seek out lunching partners among colleagues. He owned a car but would cook up reasons he could not drive. He claimed he had forgotten to bring his car keys with him and that it would be inconvenient to go back to his office. Or he said he was not feeling well and preferred to be driven, or that he would like to feel how it would be like to be driven, or just to feel the car seats to check out the comfort level, etc. There was never a time that he would volunteer to drive. He would be the first to suggest the lunch venue, avoiding food courts, as that would mean to each his own, payment included, which was not his objective. So more often than not it would be at those communal food outlets otherwise known as "zhi cha," a kind of restaurant. That would mean a single food operator dishing up all the courses under one common bill.

Going Dutch in such cases would be reasonable, but someone had to settle the bill first. He would never be one to ask for the bill, and when the bill was making its way to the table, a sudden toilet urge would give him a convenient excuse to disappear in timely fashion. Even though the per-diner share had been determined, he would declare he had forgotten his wallet. Even at food court, wherein each person would have to settle his own meal, he would ask somebody to pay first. He would settle it later, which meant . . . never! Among friends, how often does one expect reminders to settle one's share of a meal? In fact, after a long while it would be a social discomfort to even raise the matter, let alone collect. So he took this human weakness to advantage and allowed time and consequently forgetfulness to "pay" for his dues. That went on until this unsavoury trait became apparent, and all seemed to snigger at his "invitation" to lunch and avoided his company at all costs.

Then there is the "ghost host." He would call friends up to chat up old times, and sometimes it would end up meeting up for a meal. The social convention is that whoever calls is the host. But in this case it is a bit nebulous as both would like to meet, so after the meal is done, this "host" would sit back and relax and wait until the other party called for the bill to settle. A ghostly affair indeed.

Once there was this client who called up the supplier asking for a lunch meeting at 12.30. He would specify the name of the restaurant and would be there at noon, way before the host. Upon arrival, the host would be coyly told that since he had been there earlier, and since he knew the captain of the restaurant and that a certain specialty was available only during that time, he had proceeded to order the food. "Hope this is okay with you," would be the common excuse. Here is a client. He was early and had done a "favour" for you in ordering the food, so how could any supplier say no? Innocent enough, until he got hit with the bill!

Friendship is developed whenever communication and contact between parties happens on a regular basis, like in schools, where fellow students would be classed together and even be seated or grouped together. During national service it is not uncommon to find fellow recruit-mates eventually partnering up in business after their enlistment

Lesson to learn from this? Be suspicious, as lying beneath every benign demeanour there could well be a malignant animal. Such phenomena is understandable, as we are all humans, as with role changes one's relative importance to interested parties has a definite bearing on relationships and the consequence of those relationships. Should one be disappointed? I don't think so. As there are animals, there will always be people. Be guarded so as not to fall prey to artificial sweetness. No one has the right to demand that one good turn deserves a lifetime of gratitude. Be mentally prepared to avoid being disappointed. Always remember that casual friendship does not have a timeless dimension and will always be subject to human weaknesses and vagaries. This is not to say about true and enduring ones like our spouses and those who in one way or another showed their mettle and willingness to treasure the relationship.

This is a long-winded approach to touch on a very important junction that should be shared, and that is really managing oneself and the ensuing mental preparedness, lest one should find himself or herself disappointed in life. The same can be said for those who thought that by virtue of their past relationships in the office, when one embarks on a new business entity, one would be entitled to the willing helping hand from their ex-colleagues. But this is not always going to be. Do not expect any such extension so as not to be disappointed. If you do get some assistance, it is a bonus. If you adopt such a philosophy, I would say you are better prepared for life!

Make friends by all means, be nice by all means, but please manage your expectations. For from a thousand disappointments will only yield a few great outcomes.

Another situation an office or a company offers is fertile breeding ground for relationships, even marriages and sometimes affairs. Like-minded characteristics and psychological make-up in recruitment for certain job requirements would fuel this notion further. For instance, in a sales department where all gregarious creatures are grouped together, it can be expected that this multitude of similar interests and aspirations would create this "gravitational pull." So it is not unexpected that in due course relationship could be taken for granted. It is like in a marriage when both spouses after twenty years would be inclined to take each other for granted.

At this juncture, it may be appropriate to recognize that men, in general, tend to descend into the unwitting adoption of what is termed as the RR (role reversal) syndrome, the relationship process of which can be identified roughly as

1. Chase excites.
2. Conquest satisfies.
3. Familiarity assumes.
4. Complacency nullifies.
5. Relationship role inverses.
6. Competition reignites.

How often have we witnessed ageing couples in their seventies holding hands and caring for each other? Not often enough! The reverse reaction is more common, "Everybody knows that we have been married for soooo many years and as our age is also telling, there is no need to relive old moments. Holding hands and kissing in public are for the young and vibrant!"

This is true even among young couples. I have witnessed a growing phenomenon. When youngsters are in their courtship days, the men would do the chasing and there was no end to the men initiating and labouring through just to impress. Handholding is not only exciting but a manifestation of conquest, at least to men, to ward off would-be competitors. "This lady is mine, so lay off." Ladies would have doors opened for them. And men would gladly queue for hours at food courts to buy that delicious dish to impress with their new find. The men would even celebrate not their annual but their monthly anniversaries of their first meeting, sometimes complete with gifts. The list can go on and on.

However, after the hunt and the excitement of the chase are over, things would take a totally different turn. Complacency sets in and the relationship is taken for granted. Men or husbands would be seen seated at tables waiting to be served, while the wives or girlfriends would now be waiting in the queue. After all, it would have been the ladies' job to cook at home anyway. What a role reversal—RR! "Can you not open the car doors yourself? Otherwise I would have to walk over to the passenger side just to open the door for you." This will continue for as long as the other partner allows. To the female readers, my suggestion is to never allow this role reversal to happen for as long as you can help it. Start by bringing the spouse to the awareness of the development to avert any potential problem.

However, when one becomes suspicious that there are suitors for his spouse/girlfriend, that suspicion will reignite the flame of the glorious past. The fear of a possible loss is damning. Untold ferocity is awakened, some to a regretful end. Stories are aplenty bearing testimony to this fact.

Entrepreneurial and Managerial Junctions

Robert used to hold a fairly senior position in a local company with a team of about five people. Among his duties, he took care of the regional market as well. He was unquestionably hardworking. He would be the first in the office and among the last to leave. A fine gentleman, he was known to have a penchant for well-coordinated dressing. He was cheerful and slow to anger. Because of his regional coverage his network in the region grew, and before long he was offered a job to head the sales outfit in Vietnam. His perks would include a company-paid car with a driver, a house, complete with a live-in maid, with home leave thrown in for good measure.

But beneath the veneer of a hardworking and intelligent executive with a genial demeanour was one arrogant and patronizing persona. Those who had worked with him would swear he micromanaged and was often very petty. A true chameleon, he would know when to don the correct skin in any given situation or forum. With his staff, he was well known as a tough taskmaster. With his bosses there was this servitude of a demure and genteel creature. With this approach, his bosses were somewhat hoodwinked into believing that here was this hardworking executive and therefore he would make a good manager of people. A good salesperson does not necessarily a good manager make. In any case he left for greener pastures. But soon he was out looking at yet other jobs, and his ex-boss still believed in him and was prepared to dish out spotless references whenever head hunters called. So he was rolling from job to job in some senior positions, but for his condescending attitude he began to falter, just as fast, one after another.

He did not seem to learn from his failings. When a new executive is installed in a very senior position of any company and whose business is quite alien to one's background, extraordinary efforts would have to be enlisted to gain the support and respect of the staff. How does one achieve this as one embarks on the lowest point of one's learning curve for the new business, yet have to make decisions despite one's lack of know-how? For starters, one is expected to seek out as much information from the Internet, from books, and from friends to hold ignorance at bay. Staff was confronted with this unenviable dilemma—whether they should teach their new boss the business and how to manage them.

Understandably, some would resort to status quo, preferring to refer matters to the former boss or even the chairman. Instead of trying to win over the staff, Robert chose to ignore them and adopt an arrogant stance, as he wrongly assumed that as the new manager all the staff should back down and accord him the respect deserving of the position. He was wrong. Very soon no one was talking to him, and the bolder ones began insubordinating his authority. It would not be long before he lost his job, which he did time and time again.

Robert then decided to start his own business dealing with office equipment for the home. But business was not good and he was lucky to be headhunted again for another job. This time to be the MD of a food and beverage company based in Thailand.

Even before he commenced work, he demanded many perks some totally uncalled for. He wanted expatriate terms, with home leave, a chauffeur-driven car, and a three-bedroom apartment. The starting salary, which was way higher than his income from his own business, was something he felt was inequitable compensation. That was a bit mind boggling to his friend. Here was a case where his income was so low, and he had chosen to compare his salary to what he had gotten before, years ago. He was still living in his old days.

His friends could not fathom why he required a three-bedroom when he should be happy with a studio apartment. His response was that he would sleep in one, convert the second to be his study, and convert the third into a guest room. One wonders where his priorities were. Could not he study and work in his own bedroom? Why should the company cater to him and provide accommodation for his guests? If the guests were colleagues, they would be taken care of. So here was a case of an obvious self-centredness overwhelming the reality of life.

Sadly, he again had to look for another job. He said he resigned after three months, but his friends thought it was more likely that he was asked to go. All felt he was not being realistic and was still living in a world of his own.

The lesson to learn from this is that one should be practical and reasonable in seeking employment opportunities. Bring in the first dollar first, and then if the company should choose to cast a blind eye to the performance it would be their loss, as your reputation would have been the best testimony and a deserving one.

Another case. After having spent thirty-odd years in the corporate jungle, Dean decided to branch out on his own. The intention was to take a breather for three months, which was never possible in the realm of the commercial world. It had been his belief that it was not without reason that companies were obliged to grant leaves of absence to all staff members, so that the human body would be given time to relax to recharge and refresh, as continuous labour will only yield mental and physical fatigue. Exhaustion would be counterproductive for companies, as mistakes and the lack of sharpness and alertness can be costly.

So he began what he thought would be a good break. After barely one month a relative suffered a heart attack and passed on. For more than twenty-five years he had run a food-supply outfit and had quite a good clientele, which included some relatively big companies. His family decided to gradually wind down the company with the intention of closing it down. Dean and his wife felt otherwise. They thought that after so many years and with so much goodwill with a reasonable following, the company should not take that route.

It was after one-and-a-half months after his departure from the corporate jungle that Dean bought the company. The negotiation that took place prior to taking over was a lesson in itself. Remember that the intention was to close the company, so Dean thought the takeover price could not be too unaffordable and straightforward. But it was not. Humans are, after all, humans.

The following illustrates the basic principle of supply and demand and working with the human psyche. A throwaway item suddenly became valuable because of sudden explicit interest. When the offer price was quoted it was beyond belief, so the buyer decided to skip it altogether. Upon receipt of the withdrawal of the offer, the selling price began drastically dropping. It was, after all, meant to be a throwaway. So a contract was drawn up and the ownership was effectively transferred. A start date for the takeover was agreed upon, after which businesses received would rest with the transferee.

After the agreed-upon takeover date, Dean received a small piece of business from a big company. Even though this client had been duly notified of the new owners and the accompanying change of address, the cheque was dispatched to the old address despite the agreement being adequately and legally endorsed. It was only after a while that upon checking with the client that Dean realized the bill was indeed paid for and that the cheque was presented to the bank, but not by Dean, the new owner. In other words, the transferor cashed the cheque and kept the money which rightly belonged to Dean. Repeated attempts to recover this small bill from the transferor met with pleas of ignorance, and after a few tries, Dean decided not to pursue the matter any further.

Lessons from this experience? Well, for one, the value of useless items increases exponentially with demand, however small it may be. Money has the nasty effect of thinning and even obliterating the existence of blood. So to those who consider blood an integral part of a business or a commercial undertaking, please take steps to ensure that relationships will not be compromised, or at least be psychologically prepared for a possibly unpleasant outcome. Better still, avoid this "B" combination, as blood and business do not mix. If anything, it destroys relationships!

For five years, poor Bridget laboured through helping Dean run the food-supply business. She even had to drive the van ferrying the workers, looking after their welfare, and buying them lunches and dinners, while Dean doubled up with Alphadvertising. There were times Dean's sweat-drenched outfit must have been the reason he lost some business, with the stench that came with it. Dean felt it was not highly profitable if he were to scrutinize the true returns. But it was a good journey, and hard lessons yielded strong outcomes.

Dean's niece, Chelsea, was married to George, and they were away in Holland on an overseas assignment. About a year before their impending return they expressed an interest in taking over the business, and it was an excellent fit in the scheme of things. This time the transfer was a breeze. No hiccups. Chelsea and George managed the company very well and were more than happy with their decision to take it over.

So Dean had the time to fully concentrate on Alphadvertising. He had this arrangement with Bart, who would take care of the creative side while Dean looked after the business aspects. All was okay for a while.

Dean had been acquainted with Bart for quite a while, but it was on a business level. That meant they became partners on the premise of doing business, and according to Bart's definition, "Friends are more important than business," which meant their partnership was second to Bart's friends. But it can be seen as in most cases that friendship can be expected to blossom from almost any undertaking—but not in this instance.

That is one question Dean is still grappling with. Cannot the two concepts coexist? One wonders. Some people seem to think one prevails over the other.

Bart has one close friend who has had an overpowering influence and authority over him. Dean gathered that they had worked together before, and since Bart was the subordinate, the relationship continued on that basis. Since leaving the company, each went his separate way. It was also apparent that this friend had been very supportive of Bart wherever he may be working by ensuring that he would award all business to Bart. So somehow Dean was drawn to believe it was this gratitude that compelled their unequal relationship. Even when money was concerned there was a hesitance on Bart's part. That typified what could be called gritted silence.

Bart and Dean shared the same belief in being frugal and a host of other things. They did not believe in overspending and luxuriating in anything. Keeping a low profile had always been their approach to life as well as in business. Both worked very hard and tremendously enjoyed their work. What seemed to polarize them made the partnership work. Bart was an introvert whereas Dean was a gregarious animal, although Dean would be equally happy being with himself all the time.

But all good things must come to an end.

This friend of Bart's knew his employment contract with one company would not be renewed. As a contingency plan he tried to get Bart to work with him as a possible partner for another business, which would unfortunately be competing with Alphadvertising. Of course Dean objected, and as one who would not mince words and to adequately reflect his feelings and sentiments, he let fly some expletives. Dean suspected he was most accurately quoted as the sudden coldness emanating from this guy was overwhelming and that was when Dean submitted that, indeed, "Friendship is more important than business!" at least to Bart, but Dean was still in wonderment.

Lessons From Golf

After his decision to cease Aphadvertising, he chose to partake in a not-so-strenuous activity—golf—to keep himself gainfully occupied and at the same time maintain or improve on a good social network.

In fact through this he made quite a few new contacts, which even at a senior age he was glad he was able to achieve. Again, another lesson that could be learnt here is that there is no such thing as a limit to one's learning and to making new friends.

Dean's new network is a motley group of unlikely demographics, compromising high-net-worth individuals from all walks of life. Some are gentlemen with a great deal of social finesse, and oddly, he found that equally, if not more so, there are those from the other end of the spectrum. Some turned out to be good friends while others remained good weekly golfing partners. There was one golfer by the name of Sam, whom Dean came to know in the course of his game. He turned out to be a gem of a friend. He would go out of his way to obtain some herbs for Dean's daughter, travelling miles on end to achieve this. He would also offer to pick up fellow golfers to bring to the course, even though the others had a car. Gifts from him abound after most of his travels.

It should come as no surprise that sometimes much could also be achieved through golf. Some staggering businesses were concluded on the fairways.

It is also through golf that one can discover the characteristics of individuals, warts and all. The reason golf attracts a great deal of senior executives is not so much because of the perceived social status but because the game challenges oneself, which is very much part of the mental and intellectual makeup of such senior positions. Unlike most other competitive sporting activities (except, perhaps, for bowling), one's performance in golf is not dependent on the ability/inability of the opponents but on yourself. So if you don't play well, it is understandable that if and when one's game should wane or degenerate, frustration can set in. How one is able to manage and control one's own temperament during such occasions is telling about the person.

Control one's temperament during the game is only one aspect of one's character. There are the pre- and post-game episodes that can reveal oneself too.

For example, it is quite common to witness golf clubs being thrown into ponds or even being broken into two, or letting out expletives in generous doses. It was said that there were certain companies that would choose to play a round of golf before offering a prospective candidate a job, particularly those jobs requiring the person to deal with external clients or vendors. In other words, those jobs that were highly stressful. Whether the adoption of this method is correct before confirming employment of a candidate remains controversial.

Second example: It is not just one's response to one's performance during play that will reveal a person's true characters, as Dean discovered from his friend's narrative. Dean remembered this story of a group of golfers—some CEOs or the like, numbering about twenty regular golfers belonging to the same club. All were working, and the booking of the time slots for the game had been a hassle. Bookings had to be done personally seven days ahead, as required by the club, with one member being allowed to only book for four. With a group of twenty, that meant that each week five players would be required to be personally present at the club to do the task.

Initially, there were willing "bookers" for as long as there were incentives in return. In this instance, each booker would be credited with a $10 value to be used for the group's annual event. However, when this incentive was withdrawn, these regular bookers were suddenly too busy.

Third example was when there were those who would conveniently sponge off others with oft-cited excuses of having to attend meetings during the time of the booking, which happened all the time, while others plainly refused to do their part, to the extent of blatantly refusing to even agree to a roster so that all would have a fair share of the load. That's attitude for you!

Fourth example: It was not uncommon during golf to have small wagers to add another interesting dimension to the game. Remember, these wagers were no more than $20 per game, which is about 0.05 per cent of their average monthly salaries. With games that did not have wagers, you would never guess the integrity of such senior people. All were angelic. But with wagers, horns will appear even for the paltry wager. Those with magnanimous façades suddenly morphed into ugly monsters. Rules of the game will be ignored for their own benefit, but not so for their opponents', with the accompanying insistence of their wayward righteousness.

Retire?

Dean is not young anymore, so many of his friends and many freshly made encounters would enquire whether he had retired. His white hair is a giveaway. His response has been a constant, "No one should ever actually retire," as his conviction is that the more active the brain works, the more able your physical being. There is no doubt that wear and tear and biological degeneration is very much part and parcel of the ageing process, but the marvellous effects of the mind works wonders for the body. It is only through engaging oneself with mental and physical activities can one really have an enriching and fulfilling life. In fact, in the earlier part of the book this topic was accorded mention, touching on the difference between being involved commercially and in social work.

In the ensuing article from a friend, Cheng Huang Leng, you will note his salient comments on planning for retirement.

There is, however, one aspect that is not in agreement with Dean's philosophy, and that is Cheng prescribed a heavy weightage on social activities, like sports, social work, and community work with a lot less emphasis on commercial activities. This imbalance will not produce the same effect on the body as much as with commercial activities, as the brain is less engaged in this formula. His examples of MM Lee and the judges would attest to that point of view; see below.

In any case, this is Cheng's take on retirement, which is reproduced wholesale without any surgery and for which permission was obtained to reproduce it in full. It offers another alternative perspective.

How to Retire?

Four Preconditions for Retirement

I (Cheng) retired in the year 2000 at age fifty-two. I am now sixty-one, so I can claim that I got more experience at retirement than most! I thought I should share my experience with mariners because I have seen too many friends and neighbours who became so bored that they have become a nuisance to their spouse, children, and others!

A few have solved the problem by going back to work. They were able to do so because they have a skill/expertise that is still in demand. The rest (and many are my neighbours) live aimlessly or are waiting to die—a very sad situation, indeed.

You can retire only when you fulfil these four preconditions:

1. Your children are financially independent (e.g., they got jobs);
2. You have zero liability (all your borrowings are paid up);
3. You have enough savings to support your lifestyle for the rest of your life; and most importantly,
4. You know what you will be doing during your retirement.

Do not retire until you meet all four preconditions. And of course you should not retire if you enjoy working and are getting paid for it!

The problem cases I know of are those that failed to meet precondition #4.

When asked, "What would you be doing during your retirement?" some replied, "I will travel/cruise and see the world." They did that, some for three months, and then they ran out of ideas. The golfers replied, "I can golf every day." Most could not because they were no longer fit to play well enough to enjoy the game. Those who could needed to overcome another hurdle—the need to find the "kakis" to play with them.

It's the same with mahjong, bridge, badminton, trekking, and karaoke—you need "kakis"! Most could not find others who share their favourite game, and playing/ singing alone is no fun. *And* when they do find them, a few found they were *not* welcome, like my obnoxious neighbour, whom everyone avoids.

Thus if you are into group sports or games, you must form your groups before you retire. You need to identify your "kakis," so play with them and discover whether they "click" with you.

The less sporty "can read all the books bought over the years." I know of one guy who fell asleep after a few pages and ended up napping most of the time! He discovered that he did not like to read after all. We do change and may not enjoy the hobbies we once enjoyed.

Routine Activities to Fill Your Week

For most people, your routine work activities are planned for you or dictated by others and circumstances. When you retire, you wake up to a new routine—one that you have to establish as nobody else will do it for you!

The routine to establish should keep your body, mind and spirit "sharpened." A good routine would comprise:

1. One weekly physical sport—you need to keep fit to enjoy your retirement. If you are the non-sporty type, you should fire your maid and clean your home without mechanical aids. Dancing and babysitting are good alternatives.

2. One weekly mind-stimulating activity—e.g., writing, studying for a degree, acquiring a new skill,

solving problems or puzzles, learning or teaching something. You need to stimulate your mind to stay alive because the day you stop using your brain is the day you start to die.

3. One weekly social activity—choose one involving lots of friends/neighbours. Get yourself accepted as a member to at least three interests groups. Unless you prefer to be alone, you do need friends more than ever as you get older and less fit to pursue your sport.

4. One weekly community service activity—you need to give to appreciate what you have taken in this life. It's good to leave some kind of legacy.

With four weekly activities, you got four days out of seven covered. The remaining three days should be devoted to family-related activities. In this way, you maintain a balance between amusing yourself and your family members. Any spare time should remain "spare" so that you can capitalise on opportunities that come your way like responding to an unexpected request to do a job or to take advantage of cheap fares to see places or to visit an exhibition.

Mind-Stimulating Activities

Most judges live to a ripe old age. They use their brains a lot to decide cases. I am sure MM Lee's brain works overtime. He's eighty-plus and still going strong.

In *Today* newspaper, you might have read about two inspiring oldies. One is a granny who learned to play the guitar at age sixty in order to entertain his grandchildren. She's seventy-plus today, and those grandchildren have grown to play with her. Another is an Indian radiologist who, on retirement, qualified as an acupuncturist. He is seventy-seven and still offers his services (by appointment only), including free visits to those who have no income. I guarantee you they are happy people who discovered a "second wind" to take them to the sunset with a smile on their faces.

Mind-stimulating activities are hard to identify. They require your will to do something useful with the rest of your life, a mindset change, and the discipline to carry it through.

Your "Bucket List"

Despite your busy routine, you will at times be bored. Then it's time to turn to your "bucket list."

Your bucket list contains a list of things to do before you kick the bucket. They are not routine and are usually one-off activities. You need them to have something to look forward to. These include anniversaries, trips (and pilgrimages), visits to friends and relations abroad, redoing your home, attending conferences (related to your hobbies), or acquiring a new set of expertise. 4 such activities that are spaced out quarterly would be ideal.

Retirement Is a Serious Business

If you can afford to retire and want to, do prepare to live to your fullest. You need to be fit to enjoy it— therefore, get into shape now. You do not want to get up on a Monday and wonder what to do each week, so identify your set of weekly routine activities now and try them out to confirm that they are the activities you will be looking forward to doing week after week. You bucket list of "rewards" or "projects" or "challenges" is needed to help you break away from the routine, thereby making life worth living. Start listing what you fancy and refine it as you chug along in your retirement. You will have so much fun, you would wish you had retired when you turned twenty-one!

By Cheng Huang Leng

Knowing How to Behave after Retirement

Dean remembered two polarizing stories that his friends candidly shared about their encounters with their former bosses as lessons to better manage our self-esteem.

Gordon was working for Zen in one printing company. The latter was about ten years older, which meant he retired earlier than Gordon. Now that Gordon has also retired, and despite the age difference, they kept in touch, through no less the efforts and savvy of Zen.

Zen is one dynamo, and he believed in maintaining contacts with his colleagues regardless of their prior positions. That he did by continuing his tradition of organizing get-togethers on an annual basis. He would personally send out reminders to his open house parties even though all were aware of the annual function and the date. On top of the generous catered spread, his wonderful wife, Sharon, would not only play the ever-gracious hostess but would cook some favourites of the regulars.

After retirement, it is to be expected that one's contact base would shrink progressively over time, but not so for Zen. Even if it did, the shrinkage would be comparatively much smaller than the norm. One other evident characteristic of Zen was that he would treat all former subordinates as friends and as equals, to a point that the unknowing would be none the wiser. He would organize overseas trips with them and willingly share jokes and kept in touch via emails. One great boss.

Conversely, another manager by the name of Tan could never shed his egocentric and autocratic manner even after retirement. He misinterpreted social decorum as a right to persist in his distasteful manner. There was one occasion that remained indelibly in the mind of his staff that is worth repeating for readers to never fall prey to this attitude.

Tan's former subordinate (who was also retired), Edmund, was out shopping in a mall with his family, and his son was with his better half, Fatimah, who happened to be from a different race and religion. He chanced upon Tan, and out of respect he duly introduced his family and the son's friend. Tan immediately started interrogating the girl—where she was from and what religion she belonged to. This was quickly followed by an arrogant swish of his hand to show his xenophobic disapproval and he quickly strutted away, obviously preferring not to engage in further conversation. Edmund's son was understandably fuming, but Fatimah calmed him down and urged him not to descend to Tan's level of antisocial behaviour.

However, Edmund would not allow the matter to pass without doing something about it and confronted his former boss as to why he acted the way he did. Instead of apologizing or at least pleading ignorance for his wrongful behaviour, Tan let fly an expletive, as if Edmund was still working for him and therefore still beholden to him, mistakenly thinking that was his right of way. And so he thought. Tan had been well known for his colourful language and equally the ease with which he belted out the foul language even to the fairer sex, without any prompting or provocation. This infuriated Edmund, who would not accept the double insult. Tan no longer had a hold on Edmund's career, and as such he was ready to let Tan taste the raw end of his fist, his just dessert. Had it not been for some civil-minded shoppers who restrained Edmund, his ex-boss would have tasted the dirt of the shopping floor.

There will always be those who thought the gritted respect one received in the corporate world, however unworthy, would be carried forward to after retirement to his own detriment. Their presumptuous attitude would be the continued cause of their deserved social embarrassment.

The Next . . .

After completing this book, Dean went on to acquaint himself in preparation for a new journey, one that will not steer too far away from the entrepreneurial latitude that he has grown to love, and one that will be enduring enough until his brains and physical body refuse to cooperate.

But as fate would have it, Dean was approached by an ex-colleague in the production business to contribute his services as a consultant.

Between meetings, Dean squeezed whatever time he may have to partake in his other passion—golf.